"History goes on repeating itself, and so do novels, and this is a platitude, and there's nothing new under the sun."

- George Du Maurier
Trilby

It was always when Robert had a reason to leave that his boss found more reasons for him to stay. Just as he was finishing his work for the day, he saw his boss poke his bald head out from the doorway leading to the office. He knew that could only mean one thing, and sure enough, the boss came out with a muddle of papers in hand. The fat man moved quickly to put himself between his target and the time clock. Robert's blood pumped faster from his chest out to his hands; he rubbed his neck to check his pulse as his throat tightened.

"Robert, I need you to stay over," Lou announced, almost in a panic, as he waved the papers over his head and rushed towards Robert.

"I can't," Robert said. "I just worked double-time to get out of here." He clenched his teeth, and a flash of heat came over him. He hated saying no to work. The bosses rolled their eyes at it, and acted as if every excuse was a lie.

"Listen, there's no set hours here. You stay until the job is done." Acting tougher than he was, the bald, fat man crossed his arms and watched Robert.

Robert looked into the fat man's eyes and said nothing for as long as he could to show resistance, but he didn't last as long as he would've liked. "I have to make a call. I haven't had much of a break all day."

Lou nodded and dropped the papers on the table that stood between him and Robert. He scanned the factory to find his next victim and shuffled off once he was locked on.

Robert tried never to show much emotion around the bosses. He was never one to say no to work, but was always careful not to agree too readily. As long as the bosses didn't just *assume* that he would work late, he wouldn't mind doing it. He always put work first. It was a quality he prided himself on but also one that he beat himself up about when he made one too many sacrifices for a paycheck.

Without acknowledging the fresh stack of papers, he went to the break room and started a new pot of coffee before grabbing the phone off the wall. He dialed the only number he had committed to memory aside from his own and took a deep breath to calm down.

"Hello?"

"Lucy? Hey, it's Robert. How about a *late* dinner? I'm stuck here for a few more hours."

There was a moment of silence, and he could make out that Lucy wasn't alone. He heard a giggle and a whisper before she finally responded.

"You're in love with those noisy machines. When's the last time you saw daylight?"

"I go outside for smoke breaks," he said with a smile. "Anyway, I'm sorry. I can come over right after, just don't starve to death. I'll feel bad if you do."

"Don't worry about that. I'm starving already. I was just about to meet up with some people for a bite.

Come over when you get off. I'll either be here or down in the District."

Robert's throat tightened. He looked at the coffeepot and imagined throwing it across the room, with its glass breaking and steamy coffee running down the wall. "Alright" was all he could get out as his voice began to shake at the end of it. The way his voice sounded when he was upset was something he couldn't control, and he hated it. He never wanted to let anyone in on what he was thinking.

"The District should be lively tonight. There are a few bands, and I think some artists are getting together to put on a street exhibit."

"I'll see you tonight," he said, cutting himself short again. He hung the phone back up and walked over to the coffeepot. He stood in front of it with his feet planted and arms crossed as he watched the last drops come out. His anger took hold of his thoughts. It was just a few days ago that they had planned tonight's dinner. Lucy rattled off her favorite meals once, and Robert was determined to cook one to perfection. He had even cooked it all the way through earlier in the week to make sure it came out right. Some of it was still left over in the work refrigerator from yesterday's lunch. Now he felt like a fool. He thought about the people that he could hear in the background of their conversation. She spoke as if she had completely shed the idea that it was just going to be the two of them tonight. She would always be unavailable because she had plans with other people, but it seemed her plans with Robert weren't important enough to send anyone else away. He clenched his teeth while he pictured her with other people while he was stuck at work. He hated his job in these moments and wanted to walk out, but what would be the use? She was out now. Even if he got off work, he wouldn't have her all to himself. He'd rather be at work than competing for her attention with her degrading friends; they looked down on him for being an *underling*. The best he could do was get work over with as soon as possible. He hoped his absence would at least be assigned some sort of emotion from her, but he didn't really believe it.

Robert shook his head like a wet dog to rattle the thoughts out of his mind. He poured a cup of burnt black coffee and tried to accept that he was at work and away from Lucy for the next few hours. On his way out, he picked up the phone and slammed it back down into the cradle to pretend as if he had hung up on her the way he really wanted to. The action pulsed the anger out of his body like a white-hot flash from within. He made his way to his boss' office.

"What've we got out there? I haven't looked." Robert stood in the office's doorway. He eyed the chair but chose to stand, not because it would be too casual to welcome himself into the office, but because if he sat down after standing all day, he wouldn't be able to get up. He wanted to ride whatever momentum he had and just get work over with.

"It's nothing difficult," Lou said. He stopped

shuffling his papers and looked up at Robert.

Robert didn't even bother to force a smile. Exhaustion weighed down on his face. He stood there for a moment with a golf ball in his throat and wanted to speak. As he thought about what he wanted to say, sweat built up on his forehead. He never talked to a boss about what he was really thinking because he knew it would not make any difference. Bosses don't care about your home life—they spend all day at work just to escape from their own lives, and Lou was no different. He was nice enough for a boss, but you had to play by his rules. Unless you had a good story about getting too drunk and getting into some trouble over the weekend, he didn't want to hear about it. He would walk away from guys that got too personal, and those guys never lasted long in the factories.

"We'll get it done." Robert finally said. He raised his coffee mug to Lou as if it were a beer mug and walked back out onto the factory floor.

At his workstation, he was in a fury. He went back to work as if proving something to a lover he never met. He imagined a woman that appreciated a man that put work first. A woman that got aroused at the thought of hard work. A woman that thought of him all day until he returned; one that wouldn't be in the company of other people as if he didn't exist. She couldn't live without him and would never nurture suspicion. She would be a good woman for a good man.

Robert was focused; the coffee helped. But as

the night progressed, he slowly filled with obsession. He thought about his boss and felt stress. He thought about how little time he had for himself and how much time he spends in this factory. His frustration grew as much as it could until he finally had to focus it where it truly belonged—Lucy. A shock ran through him as he thought it might be true. He was obsessed with her, and mistook it for something beautiful, but now he knew—he *hated* her. He had spent the entire day thinking of her, and he was sure she'd never return the favor. She disregarded him as if he were a boring headline. All throughout the day before that phone call, he had pictured her at home in her kitchen. She would watch him from the barstool at the counter with a bottle of wine and smiling as he cooked and told stories about the crazy old men in the factories. He thought about that smile a lot; it was the only thing that carried him through most workdays.

But she wasn't thinking about him at all. That entire day, she was with someone else. Having drinks, making eye contact, listening, and laughing—all with someone else. He imagined her wasting her smile on other people and couldn't do anything about it until he got off work. He just drank coffee and worked and played out horrible scenarios in his head until he was so filled with rage and jealousy that he couldn't pour any more energy into it. His emotions went numb; what *else* could she be doing with someone else?

When work finally ended, he had to restrain himself from moving too quickly to get out of there.

If he was setting himself up for disappointment, then he was in no rush to get to it. He wanted to make *her* wait; he wanted *her* to be filled with worry the longer she went without seeing him. He imagined her sitting by the phone with a heart full of longing, waiting for his call.

When he was done lying to himself, Robert rushed to the phone and called Lucy. No answer. He poured the last cup of coffee, turned off the machine, and went outside. The night air had a chill to it that clung to the sticky sweat on his exposed skin. He lit a cigarette and looked up at a streetlight through the smoke. *It's getting late*, he thought. Part of him wanted to write her off and never speak to her again. He wanted to just go away and be alone; he was too angry to go see her and have an enjoyable time *now*. Halfway through his cigarette, he exhaled a long stream of smoke and made his mind up that he would not see her tonight. But it was the tiniest tug on his heart that overpowered his rational thought. He would do everything he could to save even a moment with her. He asked himself why he loved her so much. They were never physical aside from a few kisses he was able to steal in rare moments. Ones which she would always act as if never happened in such a way that he believed she had the power to change the past. He thought about those kisses and flicked the cigarette into the street.

He went back inside and tried the phone again, but still no answer. He took a breath to fight off any impending anxiety, but the thought of Lucy enjoying the company of another man, sometimes even just another *person*, throttled his heart into a fury. He punched the clock and went home.

The part of town that Robert and Lucy lived in wasn't much more than an outpost for the factories. Nothing built there looked like it was built with the intent of being permanent. At the edge of industry, there was a railroad that buffered the brick buildings from the homes. Lucy lived a few blocks away from the factories, where tree-lined streets blocked the dismal factory skyline from her view, but even the most charitable trees couldn't keep the negativity of a place like that from getting into people. Her house and a handful of others were the hub of the artistic community where people often met before and after heading to the bars in the District—the shopping district that once served the families of the factory workers. Once abandoned, now a row of bars that were all connected with a few art studios in between. A bar called The Bounty was the only exception; it had always been there but was separated by an old junkyard at the end of the main drag. The patrons of the District knew well enough that they were not welcome at The Bounty, but they all knew of its existence because they had to pass by it on their way to the train platform. As the pretentious waves of culture walked by, The Bounty stood and judged them. They could sense it as they walked. Their fake shells cracked under its scrutiny.

Robert lived in apartments that had been around since the factories were built. He opened the door, threw his keys at the counter, and made his way to a bottle of beer. He kicked the fridge door closed behind him and looked out into his living quarters. Inside, it was a very welcoming apartment, despite the view from outside. He couldn't understand why Lucy wouldn't stay during her first and only visit. There were books and records, plenty of booze, a fireplace, and even a balcony to smoke on that looks out on to one of the more pleasant streets that ran the length to the industrial park. He thought it was all very comforting, but she didn't even finish her drink before she left. Just skimming the titles of the books alone, he thought he had enough to talk to her about for hours. But instead of being enchanted by Robert and his interests, she left in a hurry and never came back, despite his appeals. If he wanted to spend time with her, he had to go out into the world of competition just to get a few moments. He really shouldn't be surprised; he knew how she was. It would be just the two of them, and Lucy could never give all of her attention to just one person. She needed to be some place where as many people as possible could just show up. She lived off the energy of other people.

He finished his beer and thoughts, then showered and dressed. Not hurrying at all—he was in no rush to discover what he had already suspected. He hoped it was late enough for her to get bored with the District and that she would be home by now, so he set out without calling. He clung to a small bit of hope that when he arrived at her house, she would be home and it would be just the two of them until they had lost the fight to stay awake. Lost in conversation, two souls twisting up to the heavens. If she were not home, it would be just as well. He would find her in one of the bars or go straight to The Bounty. Part of him wanted to catch her half naked with another man. He wanted a reason to be angry with her. He carried his anger with him like a friend. If she could just give it to him, at least he would have a friend in his emotions to spend the night with. Anything would be better than being alone, even if the company came from within.

Robert stood out on the sidewalk with a bottle in his hand, checked to make sure it was the right one, and took a quick inventory of his belongings. After all his emotions today, he got a sense of security from patting himself down. Preparing himself for the worst, he walked up the stairs and rapped on the door.

The door swung open before he had even finished pulling back his fist. It startled him as he suddenly went from his own thoughts on a lonely orange sidewalk to a jubilee of light and sound and a surge of energy as the warm air from within rushed him.

"Hey, Robert," Marie said, leaning her head on her arm that was grasping the top of the door. She was a tall, striking girl whose outline curved down her length. "Lucy's here somewhere. Although her consciousness may be a point of debate." She stepped aside to give him room to pass.

"Great," Robert mumbled while making his way inside. "Well, would *you* like a drink?" he asked and went into the kitchen, where he pulled two wineglasses from the cabinet and put them on the counter. Robert liked Marie, what little he knew about her, but he was always so focused on Lucy that he never gave chase to her.

"Absolutely," Marie said with a smile, and then flew up the stairs to retrieve Lucy. Robert poured a shallow portion of vodka into each glass. He lifted one and threw its entire contents into the back of his throat with a twitch of his neck. He grimaced at the burn and refilled the glass. Marie glided down the stairs. "She's alive! And much better off than we thought. She says she'll be right down. Wutcha got there?"

"Only the finest," Robert said as he handed Marie a glass. He hoped the sight of Marie enjoying his company would strike a blow to Lucy on some level. He would take any bit of emotion from her, even jealousy.

She glanced from the bottle to the glass in her hand. "If we must," she sighed. They clanged glasses, drew them to their lips, threw back their heads, and gulped down the liquor all in one fluid movement.

Robert grimaced again, and his cheeks reddened with warmth. His empty stomach caught fire, and the warmth spread through his veins. Marie slammed the glass down and smacked the table.

"I knew there was a reason I liked you," Robert said and filled the two glasses again.

"Go easy buddy, it ain't me you want," Marie said. Lucy's feet hit the bottom step on "You want." And Robert blushed at how much she may have heard of that sentence. He didn't like it that other people knew he wanted her, and he especially didn't like other people talking about it. Marie glanced from Robert to Lucy while shooting her drink. Robert acknowledged her empty glass and emptied his.

"I wasn't sure I'd make it to see you alive," Robert choked out through a cough and grimace.

"Why is that?" Lucy asked. She kept a sterile distance from him through the kitchen to the cabinet and withdrew two wineglasses of her own.

"I figured you'd be worn out from the District," Robert said as he eyed the two glasses and felt a quiver in his throat.

"I wasn't drinking too much. I promised I would give an honest, sober assessment of some of the work. Besides, some of that crowd is so boring—there's not enough booze in the world to make them lively. Too many outsiders are making their way to the District." Her tone seemed warm, and Robert's hopes grew. He paid no attention to the two wineglasses and pressed on.

"Well, you're in luck. I've brought your favorite." He handed her the bottle with the label facing towards her.

Lucy took the bottle and placed it back on the table in between Robert and Marie's glasses without even looking at it. "Ugh, I can't do any of that right now. I'll stick with wine. You two have fun, though."

His throat tightened and his forehead perspired. Mostly, he felt like a fool. Luckily, Lucy wasn't looking at him, but Marie was, and he could do without the audience. Marie could sense it and opened her mouth to announce her exit, but just then, Robert poured himself and Marie another shot. "I guess it's just you and me in this bottle together," he got it out before his voice cracked as a quiver threatened to make its way up from his throat. Marie didn't want to be a part of this any more than Robert did and accepted the drink to make herself more comfortable.

Lucy was now sitting on the couch in the living room, which opened to the kitchen. She was wearing a man's shirt that was so long on her it went past her shorts and made her look naked from the waist down. She was searching for a wine key among the newspapers and magazines that lay on the coffee table. Robert grabbed his glass and bottle and made his way towards her, eyeing the dip in the couch that would push their bodies together. As he was crossing the room, he heard the slap of bare feet hitting the floor at the bottom of the stairs. He looked over and saw someone that he had never seen before, and then looked at Lucy and saw her eyes melt in a way he had never seen before. Jealousy resonated throughout his body so strongly that he was sure everyone else in the room could pick up on it.

"There's my shirt," he said, pointing at Lucy. She smiled and stared until she realized other people were in the room. "Robert, this is Austin. Austin, Robert," she said.

"Hey, man," Austin said to Robert and reached out for a handshake. Robert said, "Hey," but shrugged his shoulders at the handshake and showed his hands were full. Austin went over to the couch next to Lucy, and as he did, their bodies pushed together. Robert's heart dislodged and fell into his stomach. He went back to the kitchen to pour himself and Marie another drink.

"Easy, cowboy" was the only thing he heard from Marie through his thoughts. He looked up and saw he had filled both glasses to the top with vodka. *Shit*, he thought, *now I have to stay long enough to finish those*. He realized his visit was going to be a lot longer than he would've liked and went to the fridge to get himself and Marie a beer each. He handed Marie hers and told her, "You don't have to finish all that."

"I couldn't put a good drink to waste," she said with a shocked look and accepted the beer to chase the vodka with. Her expression changed, and she gave Robert a look of compassion that was out of the view of Lucy and Austin. *This wasn't going to be easy*, he thought. But the booze gave him just enough confidence to go on. Robert started a cigarette, let out a puff of smoke and brought the wineglass to his lips.

Marie did the same with a comforting smile in her eyes.

* * * * *

Robert sat on the steps outside of Lucy's house. He escaped unnoticed, but didn't know where to go. He was trapped. He looked up at the orange sky and felt like he was looking up from under the flames of hell.

The door creaked open. He heard it close and then footsteps behind him. Marie sat on the step next to him. She put her arm through his and leaned her body against his, as if she could sense his torment and was trying to console him. He let out a puff of smoke and continued his thoughts aloud.

"The sky is always orange. Not even the light can escape. It bounces off the clouds and is sent right back down to us."

"I do miss the stars. I haven't seen one in months."

"The factories won't allow it. They never turn off, even when they're empty. They pump steam and smoke out so you can never catch yourself dreaming."

"The stars give you dreams?"

"They give me hope; they help me look out. You can't do that in the factories. If you look out, you might see something you like and go get it. They always find a way of killing those thoughts and bringing you right back. After a while, you're not capable of looking out, then you just stay here forever."

"You need to get out before they take away all your stars."

"It's impossible. There's nothing out there. Everywhere I go is the same."

"It sounds like they've already won." Marie lifted her head from Robert's shoulder. She retrieved a pack of cigarettes from Robert's pants pocket, extracted two, started them both, and passed one to Robert. Robert didn't even feel her hands searching him. It felt like his own hands had searched his pockets. She had a fluid way of being casually intimate.

Marie exhaled, "Come with us this weekend, we're going out past the college and camping. It will be refreshing, and you need to break free. Jack is going to come, and don't worry about Lucy. If you don't try to fall in love with her, you can actually have a good time."

"You know I can't. We work."

"If Jackboy can do it, you can, too. They can't hold you prisoner. Just talk to Jack about it. You need to get out and get some nature."

"I'll see how he's pulling it off when I talk to him. I think I'm gonna head to The Bounty."

"Well, I won't be joining you. This smoke was my night-cap; you pour heavy drinks, sir. Do talk to

Jack, you need it." Marie gave Robert a kiss on the cheek and stood up. She patted the ashes off her and went inside.

Robert didn't want the moment to end, but the coldness replaced her warmth and wouldn't allow him to stretch it out any longer. He looked back at the door and heard it lock. He immediately started thinking of excuses for the weekend. Getting away from this place would be a relief, but he didn't see the point if it couldn't be permanent. Seeing the outside world would just make it hurt more to come back.

He walked down the middle of the street under the flame sky, drank what was left in the bottle, and threw it out in front of him. The crash of glass on the pavement gave him a wave of comfort.

2

Robert woke to a slow, pulsating pain. Each pulse felt as though his skull was going to shatter. As his waking senses gained traction, he realized the pain pulsed in sync with his heartbeat and that he was dealing with a migraine. *No surprise*, he thought. He couldn't remember how much he drank last night, but he knew it was a lot. He tried to remember something from the bar, but the pain suppressed the memory with so much force that he thought he might never recover it. He waited for the strength to open his eyes and take on the piercing pain that the light was sure to deliver. He's been here before. Migraines were no stranger to him, but even with his routine established for dealing with them, he knew this was a bad one. It would take time to get up and get the pills, and then more time to find relief. Time was the only cure. He knew this, and so he waited.

As he lay with a pillow on his face, he tried to figure out what part of the day it was. He knew it was late and figured it was probably a few hours after noon. He tried to absorb whatever comfort he could. He hoped he was home and was quickly reassured of it when he inhaled the familiar scent of his own pillow—one minor victory on the long road to recovery. As the pain came in and out on waves, he could find tiny pockets of relief before the next wave hit. His method was to find pockets of relief where he could hide from the waves, then pool them together and ride the currents of relief far from where the waves mattered. Midway down a stream of comfort, panic flashed over him; the realization that he was late for work sent an adrenalized shock of pain through his skull. Instead of writhing, he jumped to his feet and ran out into the orange, late-day light streaking through the blinds in his apartment. He tried to ignore its significance and held out hope until the clock over the stove confirmed his fears. It was over an hour *after* his shift. His head was vibrating with such intense pain that he doubled over. His heart sank. He felt hollow. "Fuck," he said to the still room. He went to the sliding door that separated his apartment from a small balcony and pushed one of the blinds aside. He looked out at the bright orange clouds fading behind the skyline. The paltry light entering his apartment sent a dagger behind his eyes. He squinted to look out and came to acceptance; the sun was setting, the day was over, and he had no chance of saving it. His thoughts dispersed, clearing the way for a bolt of pain to crack at the back of his skull. Robert cringed and made it to a cabinet in the kitchen with his eyes closed. His shaking hands found their way to a familiar bottle and rattled a few pills out. He then made his way to the sink and swallowed the pills down with tap water from cupped hands. He stood breathing heavily as he gripped the edge of the sink hard enough that he was sure he could break it off. Once he steadied his breath and released his grip, he drank a few more palms of water and then splashed his face and rubbed the water on the back of his head.

The cold temporarily overrode the pain in his skull, and he used its effect to buy him enough time to get back to his dark bedroom. He sat on the side of his bed with his head in his hands. As the water warmed up, the pain returned. An odd thought occurred to him—*If he missed work, someone would have called. What was that? Something about a shutdown? Who said that last night? Someone at the bar.* He thought of The Bounty and why he was there. His mind jumped to Lucy. A charge of anxiety energized his migraine. He tried to push all thought from his mind. He brought his head up, still holding his face, and let his hands slide down so that his fingertips just revealed his eyes, and his focus went to the phone. *Call Lucy*—a stray demon thought flashed through his mind. *No, fuck, call Jack.*

Robert picked up the phone. The dial tone took him off guard, then signaled more pain to his migraine. He put his fingers to his eyes and put pressure on them, if not for relief, then at least get a physical grip on the pain. His other hand knew the numbers well enough and dialed Jack. He was glad the phone wasn't up to his ear as he heard the pulse of each number through the receiver. He listened for a voice, pointing the phone away from his aching head until he heard the ringing stop and give way to Jack. He heard something like "Hello." But wasn't sure and didn't care.

"Jack."

"Hey bud, how's that head?"

"It's rough. What... is... did I miss work?"

"No, you're good. There's the distribution shut down thing—the drivers are on strike. We told you last night. I'm guessing you don't remember. At least if you're calling me, you didn't waste the time of going down there to find locked doors." Anxiety charged through Robert at hearing this. He cringed at the things he said and did while drunk, but cringed even harder at the things he *could* have done in a blackout. He always had a fear of the unknown, and the anxiety fed on it. Jack continued, "Hah, man, are you just waking up?"

"Yeah.... trying to, but this migraine is beating the shit outa me. Alright, well, I thought I was in trouble at work. Thanks for the info."

Robert hung up; he didn't mean to so suddenly and hoped Jack didn't think it was rude. The pain of the migraine came back, and he couldn't toil with his thoughts anymore. Jack would understand. Jack always did. He never had to go back over anything and explain himself to him. Robert flopped back on the bed, and immediately regretted it once his head landed and shook some extra pain into the migraine. He held his head and drifted in and out of consciousness on the alternating waves of pain and relief.

Hours later, Robert woke as if the darkness jolted him. His stomach was hollow and his head was still sore, but the piercing pain was gone. He thought of how late it must be and tried to talk himself out of worry. The guilt of missing work still existed, even though there was no work to be had. He thought about a shower and another round of pills—the combination would knock out the lingering pain. He got up and glanced at the time over the stove on his way to the shower—*Not too late,* he thought. He might still go out and rejoin society. Once he had the migraine beaten, it would be best to leave it behind and go somewhere away from where he experienced it. He figured people would still be out by the time he was ready to leave.

In the shower, the warm water hit his head with majestic comfort. As it engulfed his head, it absorbed the last remnants of his pain and ushered it down the drain. He stood with his hands against the wall and his head under the rush of water and thought of the people he might see later. In his mind, he saw a crowd of people at one of the bars; he heard music and laughter and pictured himself running into anyone he knew, but then the face of Lucy stood out from the crowd. He shook his head and tried not to think of her. *No,* he thought. Now that the migraine had faded, he needed to think about her with a rational mind. He had to sort out his stance toward her before he set out for the night. If he saw her, he wanted to know exactly where he stood. He thought of last night: he was hurt—yes. He was embarrassed—of course. Not a lot was done or said, but how he felt about her was out in the air. Everyone in that room knew it, she probably even told that guy about him chasing her. He flashed with anger, then steadied—it didn't matter. None of the events leading up to last night mattered. What mattered was how things were going to go from now on. What did he truly think about Lucy? There was an emotion pushing against his defenses like a raging tide pushing against a seawall. He gave way; he knew he had to deal with this. Did he *love* her? Yes! He answered honestly. Concrete gave way to a raging sea. Fear struck his heart and rang through him. Every extremity went weak. "There, it's out," he said aloud. "Now what?"

You love her, that's fine. Does she love you back? I doubt it. Does she think about you all the time like this? I doubt it. Why does she even bother with me? Why answer the phone? Why spend time with me? Why make me a part of her life? She knows what I want and wants nothing to do with it. Is she just a free spirit? Does she really not know what's going on? He paused. Even in the hot shower, he feared the coldness of his next thought —*No. No, she knows exactly how I feel. She's not ignorant of it. She just wants attention, from you or anyone, she doesn't want anything serious with you.*

At that last revelation, he came out of his thoughts and back into the real world. He found he was washing himself. He let the water take the soap down the drain, and with it, he thought, he would let it take any love for Lucy. He had to be strong and make a hard decision—continue to pursue her or put an end to the whole idea of it. Through the water, he said, "cut her off." *Cut her off from your emotions. Don't let her get to you. Put up a wall between her and your heart. It's over.* The final thought sent a jolt through him. The truth of it stung. As he shut off the water, he exhaled a sigh of finality and knew it was true. He wouldn't let even the tiniest string of hope tug at his heart. He would show no emotion towards Lucy. Robert stepped out of the shower not even thinking negatively about her. He was efficient at controlling his emotions when they were finalized. One last time, he thought of Lucy and detected nothing. He was numb to her.

  As Robert dressed, he was composed and was ready to leave his apartment—it was beginning to suffocate him. The few moments of the day that he had experienced were tormenting, both mentally and physically, but he thought that in the end it was productive. He had a new outlook and was ready for a new beginning. As he peeked through the blinds and looked at the industrial lights, he let his fingers dial Jack on the phone. He sometimes didn't even notice the orange night sky, but this time, as he looked out, he forced himself to register the orange behind the smokestacks. The nighttime orange of the sky lacked the brilliance of the sunset, yet it claimed more authority as it kept vigil over Robert. He thought about the trapped factory lights shining back down to him. He drifted a little and wasn't aware of ringing from the phone until it was a few rings in, and he began to give up hope. After a few more rings, the coldness of being left out sank in, and by the time he hung up, he had lost count of how many rings he let loose into Jack's empty apartment as a full depression came over him. Depression mixed with the anxiety of missing out; it was worse than just pure depression. The thought that there was something out there as an alternative to what he was experiencing made it worse. He went out onto his balcony and let out a sigh. To process his thoughts, he began smoking a cigarette, and allowed his emotions to stir. He hated mixed emotions; they were harder to deal with. He tried to stop thinking and to let his emotions slowly drift down and settle in his chest like ashes from a volcano. With his emotions settled, he could begin his work of either dealing with them or shielding himself. He decided on this night he would go numb and forget his emotions. He would go out for a night walk, floating through the streets, immune to anything, numb to everything.

Just as he was about to fully commit to this notion, he was jolted by the sound of a knock at the door. The alarm sent through him by the sound burst his emotions out into the night. Frustration flashed over him as his mind tried to grab at a fleeting thought before he abandoned the pointless pursuit. He set his newly lit cigarette on the rail and went through the living room to the door. He swung it open to reveal a tall girl just making her way down the stairs. She turned at the sound of the door opening.

"Well, you're a hard sleeper," she said with a smile as she advanced towards the door.

"Marie! Hi! I was just smoking; I must not have heard you."

"Ah, a hard *thinker*. I didn't think you'd be asleep."

Marie entered past Robert as he held the door, and she made her way to the balcony. Robert followed as the door swung shut behind him.

She went to the rail, took in a deep breath of night air, and turned to him. "Well, good evening, Robert."

Robert couldn't respond. He had an unlit cigarette in his mouth, touching the cherry of the one he had previously started. He started the fresh cigarette in his lips, then offered it to Marie. He exhaled smoke and a response as she accepted his offering. "You scared the shit out of me. I was about twenty layers deep in thought out here."

"Well, then I came here just in time to save you from yourself."

They stood close, looking out at the night, hands on the rail with arms touching. Neither of them withdrew; they were comfortable enough with each other to be somewhat physical and enjoyed the comfortable contact in silence as they smoked and took in the lights of night. Marie finally let out a comfortable sigh and spoke first.

"I heard you're all outa work for a little bit."

He continued looking out. "That's what they say."

"I bet you had no idea what to do with a whole day off to yourself."

He glanced at her, "I spent most of it in bed, I just started the day really…"

She turned to face him. "All day in bed? Sheesh, must be nice to be a royal."

"Yes, absolutely glamorous; bedridden with migraine. I just now got over it. I need to get out of here and get some air. I'm suffocating in this apartment."

"I'm good for a night walk, but first—I come bearing gifts." She opened her purse and produced a bottle of vodka.

Robert was initially uneasy at the sight, but then his nerves settled. He would not win any argument with this girl when she was determined to drink.

"I knew it. You've come here to kill me."

"Well, sir, you put quite a hurtin' on me last night. I don't wanna hear any complaints. Let's get a little warm before we go out."

The two re-entered Robert's apartment. Marie planted herself on a barstool at the tall counter that separated the small kitchen from what passed as a living room. It was the largest room in the apartment and was minimally furnished. Robert said it helped him think more clearly with less clutter taking up space.

Robert turned on the lights that had threatened his migraine all day, and for the first time since she arrived, he noticed her beauty. He had just enough time to take in the sight of her as she was distracted by looking around his apartment. As she turned back, he dismissed the thought of admiration as it systematically ushered in the inadequacy so frequently experienced with his affection towards Lucy. He grabbed a wineglass and a shot glass and turned to look at Marie. He held them both up, waiting for a reply.

"Ok, just the shot glass, cowboy. You did want to be able to leave this apartment at some point this evening—for fear of suffocation, was it?"

Robert smirked as he switched out glasses. He put them on the bar in front of Marie and grabbed two beers to chase the vodka she was pouring. Robert opened the beers and traded one with Marie for a shot.

"Hair of the dog and all that." She raised her glass to Robert's and threw it back. She made a sound like someone knocked the wind out of her and let out, "You're a dangerous man."

"Well, excuse me, but I'm pretty sure I opened the door to the dangerous woman wielding a bottle of vodka. In fact, I think *I'm* a victim this evening."

"You brought this on yourself, and you know it. Did I ever drink like this before we met? No. did I ever even desire it? No. You, sir. *You* came into my life with all these wild ways and ideas."

"Well..." Robert smiled as he poured two more shots. "I am *truly* sorry." He pushed his offering across the bar.

She looked at him with eyes that stirred a longing for her in a quick flash that he couldn't hang on to—she took the look away as quickly as she offered it. Before he knew what to make of it, she flashed a devious smile that sliced through him again. "Apology accepted."

She slammed the shot glass on the bar and stood up to circle the room. The vodka was taking effect. Robert watched her as he tried to make sense of the scene. His emotions on the balcony never had time to settle before she knocked at his door, and now there were new ones getting mixed in. Finally, and with relief, the warmth of the vodka worked its way down the veins in his arms, then back up to his chest before warming his mind and wrapping a numb blanket around his reeling emotions. Without a fight, he let go and gave way to the drug. He made a resolve to live in the moment, and in this moment he was happy. He felt almost better than he should, in a welcome contrast to his miserable day. He adopted a sanguine disposition with what he let himself admit was a beautiful woman. Marie's presence filled the room with warm joy. Robert allowed himself to truly enjoy the present moment. He was sure that weight of his emotions was physically vacating his mind. He walked towards her with the slightest intention of embracing her, but he hadn't even made it a full step before she turned to him and spoke.

"Alright, one more of those and let's get out of here. I've got a plan; let's head down to the piers. We can grab some greasy food to slow down the drunk on the way."

He stopped mid-step; he didn't even know if his intentions were real. Didn't really know if he would have gone through with it—all this in a flash. He gave no further hesitation for her to notice as he agreed, "Sounds good to me. I'm famished."

"Me too. I could barely eat today, everything hurt. I've only smoked for lunch."

"One more for the road." They took down their drinks in unison and then finished their beers to chase the vodka away. Robert went around, turning off lights and closing doors. Marie removed her heavy outer jacket to reveal a hoodie underneath. He grabbed his keys and wallet, then put his hand up to his jacket, debating whether he wanted to take it with him.

"It was just on the brink of heavy jacket weather before those shots. The weather should hold out. Hoodies will do just fine," Marie said as she plopped her jacket on the kitchen bar.

Robert nodded in agreement and led the way out the front door. The pace seemed off. He looked behind him to see Marie fishing through her purse and then leaving it, along with the bottle and jacket, on the countertop. Robert hadn't expected that. She refrained from making eye contact as she walked past him and waited at the top of the stairs for him. As he was locking the door, he thought about how she usually just drifted off at the end of their escapades with no intention of returning to his apartment. In fact, this was one of the rare times she met him at his apartment. Their usual habit was to meet each other at a bar or run into each other on the street and then join forces for the rest of their evening out. He didn't know what to make of it, but he knew he wanted to leave it as an option, so he said nothing of her effects left behind. When he was through with the door, he turned to her and took in her figure. The hoodie she was wearing showed her form but was just loose enough that it left the intimate curves of her body to his imagination. It hit Robert harder than if it were tight and revealing. His imagination penetrated deeper into his mind than any visual image his eyes could absorb. The warm hurry of desire grew in his chest as he walked toward her.

"I'm glad you stopped by," he said, as truly as he could manage. Marie smiled before she started down the stairs.

Down on the street, Robert thought of the vodka in his apartment. He knew it was going to be a drinking night and wondered if he should bring it up that the alcohol was not with them. As if reading his mind, Marie felt a slight flutter rise in her chest and said, "We'll find something a little less strong along the way. We're both drinking on empty stomachs."

She turned before their eyes met. And with that turn, the window to any awkwardness had passed. Robert rubbed one of her shoulders, which was not an unusual gesture between them. "You have all the good ideas. I'd be blacked out again within the hour."

"Again? How much did we drink last night?"

"Hmph? No, I went down to The Bounty after we parted. I barely remember it, Jack was there."

"Ah, yes. I forgot. You know, when you're not around, I think of you as a factory worker, toiling away with the machines and breaking your back under the labor, but when I see you in person, I can't imagine you're one of *them*."

"*Them?* I didn't know you had such disdain for the men of industry."

"You know what I mean. When I think of the factories, I think of old, dirty men. Weathered by labor and drink, they fade away and tell bad jokes until their pensions come through. I don't think about what they were like when they were young. I don't know what hopes they must have had before the factories stole them all."

"You make it sound like going off to war." He said it with a touch of mockery.

"You know what I mean, Robert. I just… I don't see you becoming one of them. I don't want to see it happen to you."

"I'm not like them. The old men are alright, but they're stuck in the past. It doesn't work like you said anymore. The factories are just what we have right now, they're nothing to plan a future in. I just do it because it's what I've got right now. Besides, the old guys connect me to the past, and I like it. I like the *idea* of it, anyway. I don't plan on growing old in the factories."

"Good." And that was all that was said of it. She didn't want him to think too much about it or think that she was judging him. The mood was favorable, and she knew they both wanted to ride that wave as long as they could.

They turned the corner in the direction of the subway station, making subtle observations of their surroundings. Only about half the stores shone lights inside, but the street was lively. There were enough people walking past them and making enough noise to fill them with the energy of a night on the town. Marie ducked into a shop without saying anything. Robert followed and looked around with the face of someone trying to figure out where he was—he couldn't remember ever being in here. The interior of the shop was a combination of a liquor store, a small grocery store, and a deli with two tables. There was barely any room to breathe. Everything seemed out of place and crammed together. It got hot quick as Robert struggled to maneuver around the inventory that wasn't even on shelves. It looked like they took it straight off a truck and put it in the middle of the floor.

"Well, I was going to say it was one stop shopping, but the kitchen is closed. Anyway, we can still grab a bottle. Wutcha in the mood for?" Marie graced down the aisle as she slid a finger along the labels of the different bottles.

Robert thought of the bottle of vodka that they would surely return to and didn't want to pick out anything strong. "How does wine suit you?"

"You've read my mind. Proof those factories haven't affected all your faculties; perhaps there's hope."

"Well, abandon hope for anything but cheap wine, unless you're hiding a corkscrew on you."

"Nonsense. I am a lady, and my fine taste *shan't* be compromised." Marie had no inclinations towards expensive wine at the moment, but accepted the challenge with a touch of playfulness. Without hesitation, she grabbed two bottles of an unspecified red and walked towards the door. She dashed through the clutter of the store. Robert almost knocked down half a barrel of whiskies trying to keep up with her. He closed the gap between them and joined her at the register where he was met with the cashier's look of shock towards Marie; she had taken a corkscrew off the display and employed it against the bottles. She then stuck the corks upside down, halfway back in the bottles, threw the wine key back into the pile, and looked up at the cashier.

"Well, you don't rent them, do you?"

The man behind the counter could hold on to his mock look of astonishment no longer and let out a warm laugh. "You're lucky I like you, Marie."

She returned the smile, paid for the wine, and walked out, calling back to Robert, "Wine's on me, smokes are on you."

Robert approached and gave an apologetic look to the cashier as he pointed towards the brand of cigarettes that Marie smoked. "Two, nah... three packs, I guess."

The cashier slid the three packs across the counter, turned around, and found two cheap plastic wineglasses. "Got your hands full tonight, buddy. But she's a good one. I like Marie."

"Well, if I come back for *another* bottle, you'll know how it went."

"Hah, I know it. Take care and be careful with those open bottles—the cops are all over, lookin' for that sorta thing. The District is creeping its way up here, and with the trouble comes the cops."

"Thanks." Robert stuffed the packs each into separate pockets and grabbed the glasses. He stepped back out onto the sidewalk, where Marie was looking down towards the station.

He waved the glasses at Marie with a smile. She raised her eyebrows with a mocking expression of flattery towards a gallant gesture. Robert walked past her and placed the glasses atop a payphone. Marie smiled that he didn't throw them away.

"Only use wineglasses for vodka?" she asked, still smiling, as he made his way back to her.

"I'm sure it would look great around the cops.

Besides, the plastic makes the wine taste funny; I'll find a use for them later."

Marie stood on her toes and looked down the street. "I think I see a little activity at a food truck next to the station. It's that or we backtrack a little. Although the variety of cuisine might be gamble."

"I'm starving. Let's risk it."

Robert found inner confidence as they walked. He expected to be searching groups of people for Lucy—to be looking for her face on strangers as they passed by. But even thinking of her now didn't bring up any emotions. He looked over at Marie and appreciated what he saw. He liked her and was glad she came to the rescue these past two nights, but now he was looking at her in a different light. A fondness for her was growing. He decided it was true and was rushed with warmth as he took her in with one full up and down glance before coming up on the food truck.

"Mmmh, a little touch of the Mediterranean. The kind of food that can either hold off the effects of booze or soak it up in the morning. In our unique positions, it shall do both. I love this one. It's almost worth going out of the way to get hungover to have an excuse to chase him down."

The smell of souvlakia punctuated her words and made Robert realize just how hungry he was. There was a gnaw at his stomach and a slight ache of having nothing but a few shots of vodka on it. He was relieved that they arrived when they did. They were already ordering before he was hungry for too long.

Robert and Marie sat across from each other at a picnic table on the sidewalk. The cool night air was warmed by the smell of the food, the lights of the shops, and the chatter of people all around them. They worked at their gyros in silence, both progressing at the same pace, leaving neither to the awkwardness of waiting for the other to finish. Once they had both finished, Marie eyed the cups of water in front of them. She took one and poured it out, then under the table filled it with wine, took a sip, and put it on the table for Robert.

He smiled and drank. He wasn't sure if this was flirting or not, but he took drinking from the same cup as a good sign. She was comfortable sharing with him, not just her time but now small intimacies. He tried not to look into it too much; he was struggling with being decidedly numb this evening. He didn't want to set himself up for any more disappointment, but he knew that if anything was going to break through, it was going to be Marie.

As Marie cleared the table of everything but the cup of wine, Robert produced a pack of cigarettes and packed them. He bought her brand instead of his usual brand. A minor risk, an insignificant gesture—he wondered if she noticed. She said nothing, but as she watched him open the pack, her eyes said it all. With confidence, he put two cigarettes to his lips, started them, and gave one to her. Another victory of small intimacies. Robert was grounded; there was no unease between him and Marie. Marie took a drag and then exhaled with a sign of relief. It was all Robert needed. Whatever this was between them, they were in it together.

A thought occurred to Robert, as if trying to sabotage a perfect moment. "I thought you all were going out of town for the weekend, leaving in the morning?"

"Oh, no, not anymore. Sure, Lucy and some others are going, but they've extended it to the whole week. I have a few projects I need to finalize, I could use a weekend out with nature, but a whole week would set me back too far. You were never going anyway, were you?"

"I guess you saw right through me on that one. No, I didn't want to miss work, but even with the shut down now, I don't know—I'd have to be on call whenever it's over, besides... I need to distance myself from Lucy for a while. I've wrapped myself up in something that doesn't exist."

He didn't want to go on about Lucy and dismantle anything he and Marie had going between them. He thought that if Marie had any attraction towards him, then he had at least told her what she wanted to hear and confirmed that whatever he had with Lucy would not be an obstacle. It wasn't just important to let her know Lucy wouldn't be a problem for her, but he had to let her know that *he* had made the decision himself, that *he* knew its meaning—that it wasn't just a play towards Marie. He let it hang in the air just long enough to be heard but not discussed.

"Anyway..." Robert had nothing to say, but he at least blocked Marie from adding to any discussion of Lucy. Beads of sweat formed on his forehead as he searched for words, but decided the small diversion would be enough to redirect the conversation and kept silent. He watched the diffusion of the lights as he blew smoke up towards them. A puff of smoke from Marie joined his. He watched the smoke churn and mingle before he followed its source and brought his gaze down upon her. He followed her eyes to the other side of the street behind him where she was watching a group of drunk guys trying to hold on to each other as they made their way home. He got up from his side of the table and sat next to her. They shared the wine as they watched the scene unfold of boys falling over each other. It lightened the mood and washed away any hang-ups about Lucy from both their minds.

Halfway through their second round of cigarettes, they finished their cup of wine. Marie stood and drank exactly half of the remaining wine before handing it over to Robert. He finished it, tossed it in the trash, and stood. They were in sync—their timing perfect. What remained of their cigarettes would last right up to the entrance of the train station. As they approached it, they both flicked their butts at the gutter and watched as they bounced with sparks, collided in mid-air, and then fell through the grill into the abyss. Robert and Marie were not only in sync with each other, but with the very fabric of the universe.

Robert withdrew his metro card from his

wallet and swiped it at the turnstile. Marie, realizing she had left everything at Robert's, jumped close to him and pushed her body against his to pass through as one. As she did, she put one arm around him in a quick embrace. Robert could have melted, but it was over before it started. He looked back and smiled at her to try and hold on to the moment. *They were in this together*, he thought again. After the cold crept in where the warmth of her body had been, he tried to evoke the sensation back into existence and psychically experience it for as long as he could. They walked down the platform as near to each other as they could get without him putting an arm around her. As soon as they came to a stop at a bench, the pings of a train coming down the rails could be heard. The silent platform was rushed with sound, first of the train rolling towards them, and then the air was filled with life by the conversations of everyone getting off the train. This was a residential stop, and most people were ending their nights; when Robert and Marie entered, they were only sharing the car with a few other people, randomly dispersed, and were far enough away that it gave them the privacy of having the car to themselves.

Robert eyed the map of line stops above the seat across from him. Five stops and the line ended down a peninsula with an unmaintained light house. He laughed to himself at the gesture. The lighthouse should be replaced with a smokestack. There was nothing touristy about where they were going, except a failed attempt at a carnivalesque boardwalk with its few shops probably closed this time of night, anyway. Both being people watchers, they remained quiet as they rode. In between moments of glancing at other passengers, they both took in the sights of the outside world passing them by; cheap housing mixed between small industry with the occasional alley going straight out and giving them a peek into the lives of the locals. Mostly repair shops and bars, with the occasional drunk walking to their home or anywhere. Just as fast as the veil was lifted, it dropped again, and a deluge of smokestacks and factories dominated their vision for the rest of the ride, aside from the tunnels preceding most of the stops. Marie took in as much as she could stand of this sight and then turned towards Robert with endearment. As she watched him take in the sight of industry, she wondered what it meant to him and how he related himself to those factories. She worried for him; she didn't want to see him turn into a lifelong factory worker. The factories could take someone beautiful and turn them dreadful the same way the factories turned beautiful landscape into a Brutalist empire. Not until the factories passed and gave way to the sight of water did she turn and look back out the windows. The train slowed and screeched as it entered the station at the end of the line—the Bowery Piers. Robert and Marie exited the train car and realized they were the only people left.

"End of the line," Marie said. The words of finality brought a sense of comfort to her; Robert relished the way he absorbed them. The two walked through the station as if they were the last two on earth; two that owned the city of an unsure apocalypse. They caught a ride on an escalator that extended up towards infinity.

Marie looked up at the ceiling. "I love this station. It's like a cathedral under the sea with the water pressure pushing down on us."

"They didn't think too much about commuters when they built this part. It was originally for freight and then converted as an afterthought. We have to come out from under all the other industrial rails that feed the factories before we get to the lobby. I think they really only built this part for the few workers that have to come down this far."

"Have you ever had to work out here?"

"No, I've been here a few times out of curiosity, just to kill time on the rare occasion that I get a full lunch break. I like to look out over the ocean and imagine what's out past the horizon. I've never been here at night, though."

"That's funny. I've only ever seen it at night. It's a bit of a secret oasis of mine; a place where I can walk and be alone, where no one will find me."

"I knew it. You're taking me out here to kill me."

"Yes, but first I need to get you drunk to make it look like an accident."

They stepped out from under the canopy of the concrete station to be greeted by a long corridor of brick and mortar. The street was empty, and the air was still. The tall buildings insulated them from the ocean winds. They were alone, save for a few utility workers that didn't even acknowledge them.

They walked under the last security camera. "Finally, we can drink." Marie withdrew the two bottles from the black plastic bag and gave one to Robert.

As they made their way to the sea, Robert uncorked his bottle and looked down the street behind them. "Looks like we're the only ones with a sense of adventure this evening," he said.

"I'll drink to that." They crossed bottlenecks with a clink and drank freely in the open, as there were no cops in this part of town. No residents to call and complain, just workers who were probably half drunk themselves, toiling away at their night jobs. They walked down the street through the valley of brick until the rows of massive buildings ended abruptly and gave way to the sound of waves and the brisk smell of sea air. There was the boardwalk that went some length down the beach, but there were no tourist attractions lining it. It was in disrepair and had dunes of sand randomly dispersed about. They walked its length until they came to a seawall that jutted out a few miles. They made their journey out into the sea mostly in silence, allowing the wind to stir in their ears. The persistent breeze ran a chill through them and compelled Marie to seek refuge under one of Robert's arms and pressed against his body. The sky lost its orange hue and transitioned to a light, moon-lit gray as they left the coast behind them.

They almost forgot about each other in their silence as their thoughts projected out towards the surrounding darkness. At last, they approached the end, at which a defunct lighthouse stood like a sentinel keeping watch over the horizon. A solitary orange streetlight illuminated a picnic table that seemed like it was placed there just for them.

"Well, that *is* convenient." Marie took a seat on the table with her feet planted on the bench as she looked out towards the horizon. Robert assumed his position by her side, despite the lighthouse shielding them from the wind.

They sat together, taking in the sights of titanic, slow-moving cargo ships coming in and out of the man-made harbor. The factories spilled in from the opposite coastline that ran parallel with their sea wall, almost stumbling over one another in a race towards the sea. The lights of industry sparkled and danced among the waves. Apart from this scene, a paramount apparition revealed itself; far out beyond the factories, ships, or any sign of industry, just above the horizon, a cluster of stars began to shine through a void in the clouds. Robert saw the stars shining through and was startled, as if a lover stepped out of a crowd. "The stars. Is this why you brought me here?"

"Yes. I wanted you to see them. This is the only place for miles that you can see them. It's been my secret up until now."

They sat overlooking the sea, their souls intertwining and beaconing out towards the patch of revealed heavens. Warm with wine and good spirits, they had no need to speak. Identical thoughts and emotions were being conjured up in both of them. They sat in telekinetic agreement, watching the ships toil away until an odd sight knocked them out of sync: "There normally aren't this many ships, and none of them seem to be moving as much as they usually do."

"It's the strike," Robert explained. "The ports are refusing to unload any of the ships. They can't go anywhere. Any movement we see is probably just them rearranging the ships so that the most important cargo gets unloaded first whenever the strike ends. It'd be interesting to see what this looks like a week from now."

"Ah, the insider's perspective. You could have left me here believing they all decided to tie up together and throw a party."

"I'm sure there's a party on more than one of those ships. The crew still gets paid, it's the land workers holding them up. They're all still on the clock until this thing is over."

A group of clouds moved in and covered the patch of stars off in the distance. The fleet of ships was drifting closer to them, causing too much noise and cluttering their view. The moment had passed. Marie stood, held her bottle to the streetlight, and saw that she had maybe half left. Robert did the same to the same result.

"Well, if we stay seated, the wine will get the best of me. Better keep moving and burn off some of this booze." She looked him in the eye. "I'm glad you got your stars tonight."

Robert stood and put his arms around Marie. Her body pressed against his made him whole. She returned the embrace and pressed their bodies together further still, with the side of her head against his. He took a deep breath and let her scent fill his lungs. He was sure she could feel his heart beating rapidly against her chest, but didn't care whether she took notice. Nothing could be more right in the world than to be with her. He rubbed his free hand up and down the center of her back to punctuate the embrace with endearment before they parted. They stood back and looked into each other's eyes with relief and adoration. Marie smiled and threaded her arm through Robert's again as she pressed the side of her body against his. Together they walked the length of the seawall and returned to land as one, not speaking much, only telling the other of something trivial that they could pick out from the industrial setting and bringing it to the other's attention. They paid no attention to direction, yet somehow ended up back at the train station just in time to deposit their empty wine bottles in the trash can at the entrance.

This time, at the turnstile, Marie plucked the metro card from Robert's hand. She ran it through the machine, turned around to face him, and then held him close as they pressed their bodies together to pass through. As their bodies parted, she smiled and ran a warm hand down his cheek. She broke free and took the lead towards the train. Robert smiled to himself as he watched her figure sway in front of him. As their bodies drifted apart through the tunnel, their thoughts of each other were closer than they had been all night. They drifted together again and joined arms halfway down the tunnel.

The subtle euphoria was only momentary, and they had realized something was wrong with the trains by the time they made it to the platform. They were greeted by empty rails and the slight smell of smoke. Robert stood at the edge of the platform and tried to look down the tracks toward the inbound tunnel. He noticed a faint haze rising out of the tunnel and spilling towards the ceiling.

"Well, it doesn't look like we should stick around here. We'll have to walk to the next station."

Marie followed his eyes to the ceiling and watched the haze forming around the lights. "That doesn't smell like any fire I've been around. It smells... industrial."

"It can't be anything good," he said as he looked back towards the way they came. "Let's get outa here."

Their sense of nervousness shattered any mounting desire between them; the nerves of their emotions broke through the layers between them and were exposed to the outside world again. But as they set up their defenses, they were sure to include each other. It brought them closer together and solidified them as a single unit against whatever the outside world might bring.

They exited the station at street level once more. The concrete canopy that jutted out towards the skyline and unveiled the beauty of the megalithic industry this time gave way to the sterile, Brutalist maze they found themselves in. They took off on a brisk walk towards the next station, Robert with his arm around Marie, and she with her gaze set out straight ahead in search of anything out of place. The sound of glass breaking startled her as her eyes bolted towards its source. A figure a block up jumped and ran, revealing a half-done graffiti mural on the side of a building. Its message was unclear, but had a slight sense of anarchy in its shapes.

"It wasn't us that startled her," Marie said without concern, but with a sureness that something was in store for them.

"No, and the smell from the station is getting stronger." Robert stopped and turned his ear to the streets. "Do you hear that?"

The flick of Robert's tongue against the roof of his mouth at his final word seemed like it set off a chain of chaos. The sound of a stampede echoed off the buildings across from them. First the sound of heavy footsteps and then shouting and the hollow sound of tear gas cannisters being shot. A mob turned the corner and was heading towards them.

"In here!" Robert pulled Marie's body into the doorway of one of the nearby buildings. He pulled his hood up over his head and down as far as it would go on his face. He unzipped his hoodie and engulfed

Marie as he pressed their bodies against the building. He pulled his shirt up over his nose and pulled at Marie's.

"The tear gas," he muffled.

She understood and tucked her face down into her hoodie. The sound of the mob rushed by them; a dizzying array of shouting, broken glass and bricks hitting concrete, and the sound of police in pursuit. The sound faded into the distance, and Robert continued to hold Marie as he lifted the hood from his eyes. He saw the light fog of tear gas lift from the streets and a few straggling police officers idling around. His defenses retreated, and he took in the warmth of Marie for a moment. She caressed a forearm that was still tense around her before lifting her head and looking out to the street.

"Do you think they'll be back?"

Robert, realizing he was being selfish in the moment, loosened his grip on her.

"I don't think so. Not the way the cops are all standing around." He stepped onto the sidewalk and arranged his disheveled hoodie back into shape and then put a hand towards Marie. She took it as she stepped down off the stoop and kept hold as they walked down the street and around the corner to the source of the chaos.

The cops noticed them for the first time. The closest shouted, "You two!"

"Yeah?" Robert asked without much care.

The cop walked towards them before another grabbed his shoulder and spoke to him. He nodded his head and turned away from Robert and Marie.

"Great, they're gonna think we had something to do with this," Marie said as she watched the cop back down and pay them no attention.

"Nah, we'll be alright. The other saw we didn't have gas masks on, we don't look like the mob. Either way, let's get to the station before one of them gets rowdy."

They turned another corner and saw the tunnel smoking and steaming as the firefighters were still working on it. Police were barricading the scene as a crowd was materializing from nowhere.

"Well, at least we're not the only civilians around here; no mistaking us for the protesters again. Wanna take a closer look and find out what happened?"

Marie didn't respond, but kept walking and looking in the scene's direction until they reached the barricade with the other onlookers. The fire looked like it was contained to a few freight trains. The remnants of charred train cars showed it spread to the commuter rail leading into the station. The building seemed intact, and the fire was under control before it could do any more damage. She looked up at the wall above the tunnel. She couldn't make it out, but there seemed to be fresh graffiti in the style that they just passed before the mob overtook them. It must have been a message from the protestors painted across the entire span of the tunnel, but it was now blackened by soot.

"What happened?" Robert asked an officer.

"Nothin' you need to worry about. Move along."

"How am I supposed to move along when that's the station I need?" Robert pointed to the scene behind the officer.

Without looking behind him, the officer responded, "The next station is open. Walk."

"We just came from the piers. That's another thirty minutes of walking."

"Does it look like this station is gonna be operating anytime soon?" The officer looked over some heads towards a man with an orange vest on who wasn't a cop or firefighter. "Hold on." He went over and spoke a few words while motioning his head towards Robert and Marie. The officer and the man approached the barricade. "This kind man here is a rail inspector. He's on his way to the next station. You can hitch a ride with him." The man nodded in agreement.

Robert was expecting more hassle than charity. "Oh... thanks..."

The three made their way toward a pickup truck emblazoned with a railroad emblem. Behind them, the officer sarcastically muttered "... to protect and serve" before he went back to work telling the forming crowd to disperse.

"What are you two doin' out here, anyway?"

the man asked as they made their way to the truck.

"Just out for a late-night walk," Marie said.

"These goddam protesters are gonna give me a stroke before I get a chance to retire. They couldn't wait a few months to start this shit? You're not a driver, are ya?" he asked, turning to Robert.

"No, no. I run one of the machines. Outa work at the moment 'cause of the drivers."

"Good to hear, but you're a long way from The Bounty." They climbed into the truck with Marie between the two men on the bench seat in front. The man started the engine and advanced toward a railroad access road, where a cop opened a barricade to let them out.

Robert picked up the conversation once they were on their way. "The Bounty put enough of a hurtin' on me last night. Fresh air tonight was a much better choice." He glanced at Marie and then turned his attention back to the driver. "What's this all about, anyway? Fires and near-riots seem like a bit much over putting a few drivers out of work."

"Ah, it's not just drivers. A lot of the rail workers are gonna get affected too. I'm guessing it was them that started the fire, or at least they let someone in to start it. That's the only way they got in."

"Well, what do the rail workers have to do with the drivers? I thought they'd have more work when this is all said and done."

"The drivers are only the beginning, and the

rail workers are seeing it. This is just a sign of things to come. Most drivers will lose their jobs to automation, and the jobs that are left won't pay nearly as much. But the automation isn't going to stop anytime soon. In fact, as it takes on more work, there'll be more money to upgrade it. This will automate everything, including the jobs of the rail workers. Hell, the freight trains don't even have conductors anymore. Soon it will be machines and robots handling all the freight from the moment it comes off the ships until it hits yer machine. And I'm sure they'll find a way to get rid of the humans on the ships and make your machine run itself. We all knew it was coming one day; there was always a lot of talk, but it had the air that rumors always have—it seemed like it was out in the distant future and would be someone else's problem. This threat on the drivers is making a lot of people realize the future is sooner than they think."

Robert let out a sigh as he watched the stacks of international shipping containers pass by out the window. "Great… sounds like we'll be dealing with this for a while. Mind if I smoke?"

"As long as you're sharing."

Robert shook a cigarette up past the others in his pack and extended it to the driver. He then took two, started them at once, and handed one to Marie. He and the driver both cracked their windows in unison to let in some fresh air.

"What about you?" Robert let out before an exhale of smoke. "The machines gonna take your job?"

"Ah, who knows. I'll be drawing a pension by then, and I won't care. But if I were your age, I'd be looking for another means to make a living."

"Good luck convincing him of that." Marie pushed smoke out across the dashboard, and the driver cranked his window fully open to let the smoke out.

"So, you're a company man, eh?"

"As long as they pay me. I'm in line for maintenance, anyway. I don't care how many machines take over; they'll still need someone to fix 'em."

Marie hadn't heard this before and suffered a fresh heartache as she held her gaze straight out in front. Sorrow tugged at her heart with the thought of Robert *still* working in the factories long after they were automated.

"Smart man," the driver said. Marie tried to block the thoughts in her mind from ruining the night. She put a hand on Robert's leg and gave it a soft squeeze. It pulsed the emotion out of her, and she hoped it would resonate within Robert.

They drove in silence for a while on the service road that ran along the tracks. Robert watched the rails run by as Marie watched the buildings and power lines pass on either side. Marie stretched her body across Robert as she reached over to flick her cigarette butt out the window. A flash of warmth ran throughout his body as her hip pressed against him. As she returned, she made close eye contact and passed her lips close enough from his that he could sense their heat. As she plopped back down into the middle seat, they came to an abrupt stop.

"This is you," the driver said, pointing at a green and rusted door at the top of concrete stairs. "That's the utility entrance. It's open, you'll see. You'll come out on the platform between the benches and all the advertisements."

"Thanks," Robert and Marie let out in unison.

"How about another smoke for payment?"

Robert let Marie out and then ducked back into the truck to hand the driver a few more cigarettes.

"Good company man, I hope it all works out for ya with all this shit goin' on."

"Who knows. Worrying about it won't make much of a difference. Thanks for the ride." Robert backed out of the passenger side and closed the door with a wave before turning back to Marie. They could hear a train through the concrete walls and rushed up the stairs. They were shocked at the transition through the door, from the dark industrial settings outside into the brightly tiled interior at the platform of the station. But the shock had little time to take hold as they rushed again onto the train and sat.

"Is this even the right train?" Marie asked as the doors closed and the train began to move.

"Well, it sure can't go toward the station we just came from."

They made the journey home in silence, each

thinking about the consequences of the strikes and protests. Robert would be out of work indefinitely. Marie wouldn't be affected much by it other than how Robert would react, but she empathized with the workers.

It was long known that the machines were jeopardizing the futures of the working class. The town they lived in was already in shambles compared to what it used to be. The only thing that really saved it and added any life to it was the apocalyptic appeal it had to the art students like Marie. Otherwise, it would just be wasteland that served as a barracks for the people that worked for the factories. Marie wondered if she was part of the solution or the problem; was she helping a town or exploiting it? She enjoyed her surroundings and didn't think it was at the expense of anyone, but should the downfall of a class serve as an aesthetic? She didn't want Robert to think that she was taking advantage of him, that she saw him as some sort of diamond-in-the-rough charity case. She truly cared for him and saw him as something separate from the factories and what they stood for. She saw him as one of her own who got caught up in a system that had nothing to do with him. There was beauty in how he navigated through his world; she held an artistic reverence for him as he processed and interacted with his circumstances.

Robert, in contrast, wasn't thinking so profoundly about it all. He watched the factories and machines roll by the window with indifference.

Looking at the factories was the same as looking into a mirror. He had always known a connection with them, a sterile interworking that was projected back to him by the megalithic structures. They watched him, he thought. As they towered over him, they didn't make him small; they empowered him as if he were a part of something much bigger. He had no actual plans of moving up the corporate ladder of the factories, but he also knew he would not end up beaten by them. He would not grow old in the factories and sacrifice his life to them. He had always had a sense of being bigger than he was, and as he looked out the window towards his world, he saw himself as even bigger than industry. They were working for him instead of enslaving him. It was a sense that the world had to operate as it did in order to serve him, from even the smallest interactions up to the biggest industries, including things he didn't even know about, all had to exist to make his world. And that was just it—the world around him existed solely for him. As long as he used it to fulfill his purpose, everything in it was his. Everything that affected him was meant to be that way. All he saw was meant to be seen by him. Every sound was meant to reverberate within him. Every emotion was interpreted and recorded. It was not with pride or ego or with an idea that he was better than the world around him. It was with a modest humility, a deeper *knowing*, that the world as he knew it was a world that absolutely had to exist in order for him to realize his potential. His world was his connection to the universal truths that define us all.

Although he was filled with a sense of a greater purpose, it wasn't as if he saw himself as some sort of savior. He wasn't here to be famous, rich, or genius. He was here to live his version of life as perfectly as one could under the circumstances. It didn't matter how others viewed him or rated his success. *Success,* as others would define it, does not result in some wildly magnificent recognition. It results in a oneness with the universe, a deeper connection with truth and knowledge of one's self. Success is uniting with one's destiny, for better or worse.

A perfect failure is still perfection, Robert thought.

Marie clung to Robert as she worried for him. She worried he was filled with potential that was being worn down by a system he could not control. Her sympathy unhinged her soul, and she let it intertwine with Robert's.

As if sensing her thoughts, he spoke: "A perfect failure is still perfection."

The words unhinged parts of his own soul and allowed for Marie's to further fuse with his. The warmth of her spirit melded with his own. Their eyes met and souls spun together as the train came to a sudden stop. They sat in silence as the doors opened and waited a few moments before rising. They followed the tunnel up to the street, where most of the shops from earlier were closed and only a few lights and advertisements lit the way. Robert reached to the top of the pay phone and grabbed the two glasses he had left earlier. They walked the streets at a leisurely pace before arriving at the stairs to Robert's apartment, which they ascended in tandem. After unlocking the door, Robert turned to Marie, caressed a hand under her chin, and kissed her. A rush of emotion and exhilaration rose in both of them and erupted in electricity where their mouths met. The energy almost brought forth tears in both their eyes as they parted and looked at each other with august regard before embracing again.

They let the moment standalone as they entered the apartment. Marie separated from Robert to go into the kitchen. "Well, the protestors dismantled just about anything the wine did for me," she said as she grabbed the two wineglasses from Robert and rinsed them under the sink. Robert watched her from a barstool at the counter. "And what do you propose we do about that?" he asked.

Marie answered with only a smile as she dried the glasses and Robert slid the vodka bottle across the counter towards her. She motioned her eyes towards the record player. "You're on music duty."

Robert didn't hesitate. He crossed the room straight towards the shelves, pulled out a record, and put a needle to it. He then went into the kitchen, brushing against Marie while sliding a hand across her lower back before he withdrew two beers from the fridge and opened them. He went behind Marie and pushed his body against hers as he put the bottle in front of her and put his free arm around her waist. His chin was upon her shoulder, and, with the scent of her hair occupying every breath, he held and watched her fill the wineglasses. He then went back to his original place at the counter as she slid a glass to him. "Here we are again."

"Yes, and under much better circumstances," Robert said aloud, although it was addressed to himself. He rose a glass to hers, and they both took a measured shot.

Marie slapped a hand down on the counter in the same fashion as she did the night before, and they both laughed. After easing the height of emotions that had risen between them throughout the night and shedding their concerns brought about by the fire, they were able to continue the rest of the evening with a sense of passion. Marie walked around the counter and placed her wineglass before Robert as she made her way to the living room behind him. As he looked down at the two glasses, he sensed her behind him while she took off her hoodie, threw it on the couch, and then stretched out her arms above her head. As her arms came down, they found their way to Robert. One hand stroked the center of his chest as the other caressed its way down the length of his arm before she took hold of her wineglass. She stood back and held her glass towards him, commanding them to take another shot. They drank in unison. Marie backed away further and spun towards the sliding door overlooking the town as her waist began moving in rhythm with the music. Robert stood and then crossed the room to take her in his arms. Their desires took charge and cast a spell upon them for the remaining hours of the night, igniting their souls in direct contrast to the sterile industrial town as they sparked and intertwined once more in a rush towards the heavens. In a manifestation of their celestial dance, their bodies intimately united as one while the evening gently gave way to dawn.

3

In the late morning, Robert was the first to wake from the cold. He found his arm still wrapped around Marie. He withdrew it slightly and caressed the soft skin of her back with his fingers as he let his mind wander through comfortable thought. Once the fog of night lifted from his mind, the first thing he registered was the smell of the outside air. He pulled a blanket over Marie's bare shoulders and then went to the other room and closed the sliding door that led to the balcony; they were too enchanted by each other to think of closing it last night. The thought made him smile. He stood at the glass door, taking in the cold gray morning. He thought of the railcars on fire. They were probably smoldering piles of ash by now, but the commuter trains were probably running their normal schedule. He figured the cleanup from the fire might at least give a few guys some work for the week if they were willing to be cast out as strikebreakers, but if the workers were already burning train cars the first night of the strike, they probably wouldn't be too kind towards any scabs. He thought of the small mob that ran past him and Marie last night. *They all wore either ski or gas masks, but did any look familiar? Any sound familiar? It was a mob, but did anyone's figure or stance stand out? Did any voices resonate with those he knew?* He couldn't decide. It had all happened so fast, and his attention had been focused on Marie last night. He smiled again at the thought of her. He was afraid to let his defenses down to let her in, but something about her told him he would be safe. The attention she gave him wasn't out of charity, but of a genuine interest in him.

Marie came out a few moments later, pulling a shirt over her head. "Now, what could you possibly be thinking about first thing in the morning that's got that serious look on your face?" She startled him out of his thoughts and joined his side, a hand slowly rubbing between his shoulder blades.

He continued to look forward. "Ah, I don't know. The workers, the fires, the future. Train cars on fire on the first night out of work—this could get serious."

"What happens to someone like you when there's a strike? You're not in one of the groups directly affected by automation."

"I'm not sure. There hasn't really been an official union since this town started falling apart. It's been a generation since they've even paid dues, at least." Robert looked out towards the smokestacks in the distance. "Everything is unwritten. We've always just banded together with an unspoken bond. I don't even have a lease for this apartment. I just pay the factory worker's rate each month. Everything was set up so long ago that today we just go with it. Nothing is official, it's just assumed."

"But what will you do?"

"I'll go down to The Bounty or around town and check in with the guys. They've got to be congregated somewhere. There's nowhere else to go."

"You're not going to get caught up in any trouble, are you?"

"Hah, I hope not. I don't *think* this is my fight. Union or not, we stick together, though. I should show my support, pony up whatever cash I have and help out if anyone needs it."

Marie's heart sank at this last statement. She chose her words carefully. She didn't want to see Robert get stuck in this way of life. She wanted to see him break free. "Well… I do admire the sense of community. Just be careful, you don't have to sacrifice your future so that some old factory man can get his pension."

Sensing a difference of opinion, they both wanted to change the subject; neither of them wanted to put a blemish on their memories of last night, especially at the beckoning of the factories that towered over them every day.

"Got any smokes left?"

"I think there's a pack on the counter."

Marie retracted her hand and gave Robert a slow kiss on his neck before walking to the counter.

The thrill in him stormed out any thoughts of unions, fires, or miserable old men with their pensions. He broke his scrutiny of the smokestacks and what they represented and turned his attention to Marie. He watched her as she glided across the room. She retrieved the cigarettes, and then, conscious of his watching, she looked up to give him a smile. She began to walk back, but hesitated.

"How's your hangover?" The slowness of his reply was all the answer she needed. She went to the fridge and grabbed two beers before gliding back past Robert and out to the balcony.

"Wow, it got cold!" She handed Robert the beers and cigarettes and went back in to retrieve their hoodies and a blanket.

The two sat outside on an old futon with a blanket over their legs. Their bodies were pressed together, more for heat than romance. Marie started two cigarettes and then gave Robert his, along with the lighter, to open the beers. They sat in silence with the smoke and drink, working away at their hangovers. As they both dwindled down to their last savors, Marie broke the silence.

"Well, this will have to do for breakfast. I've got some work to do in the day hours. Why don't you come by this evening?" And she added, in case any remnants of Lucy were still in his mind, "We'll have the house to ourselves."

"I'll be there, barring any riots that I may have to take part in. I'm gonna see if I can find Jack and see what's going on with work."

"Don't tease about riots. I don't have any intention of trying to change the course of your life, Robert, but I really do think you're better than those factories. I won't say any more about it, just think about it sometime. Those machines aren't worth your life."

"I was just kidding, but I know. I know."

"Alright, well, I think one more beer on a less serious note will knock this hangover out for good."

Marie went back inside and began to fully dress as she searched out and collected her belongings for a quick departure. She gathered them on the counter close to the door as Robert cleaned the remnants of last night from the apartment and filled a trash bag with empty beer bottles and cigarette packs. She took a planner from her purse and looked over a few items as Robert took the last two bottles of beer from a case and folded the box into the trash bag. He opened them and led Marie back out to the balcony.

They sat again in silence, but the mood was much more joyful and absent of any thoughts of the factories. Nothing had to be said between them to manipulate the mood of the day. It was a brisk morning, now turning bright as the sun illuminated the seemingly forever-present cover of clouds that hung over the town. The usual sounds of the factories were still present, but they seemed muffled. They would never be fully silenced, even with no one occupying them.

Marie thought aloud, "It quiet. It's never this nice."

"I know. It seems like the town is asleep. There's usually such a charged energy."

"It's strange but makes me glad to see it like this, even just this once."

"It's like a dream."

They let the idea of living in a dream soak in as they spent the rest of their time together in silence. Marie took the last drag off her cigarette and deposited it into her empty beer bottle with the announcement: "Well, time to go out and face the day." She stood and folded the blanket before going inside.

"If we must." Robert stood and followed her through the apartment as she grabbed her belongings.

She slid the bottle of vodka away. "Imagine the sight of me wearing yesterday's clothes with a half-drunk handle of vodka. Keep it here or bring it by tonight." She opened the door and turned to Robert.

She put an arm around him as he wrapped his around her lower back and drew her closer. They pressed together and drew in each other's warmth.

"See you this evening?" Marie asked.

"You will."

She pulled back and released her grip as he eased his. She ran a warm hand down his cheek as she looked into his eyes, then turned and let the door shut behind her. Robert watched the door, lost in thoughts of Marie, until her lingering warmth gave way to the coldness of solitude. He pushed the door the last inch until it latched and then went to the phone in the bedroom.

He rang Jack to no answer and then went to the kitchen to check the time on the stove. It wasn't quite time for The Bounty to open, but then it never really had regular hours; it opened whenever the owner stumbled out of bed and made it to unlock the door, if he remembered to lock it at all the night before. Robert figured he would take a shower and then make his way into town to locate the troops.

As the hot water ran down his face and evaporated the loitering morning fog from his mind, Robert positioned himself within the movement forming at work. He didn't want to have to go through the hassle of finding another job; he had only been living and working in this town for a couple of years. He decided he would unite with the other workers against whatever opposing forces the factories manifested. While the others were on strike, he wouldn't work. He would stand with them. He wouldn't be making any money, but it would be worth it in the end, once everything returned to normal. He wanted this to be over with as much as anyone else, but something in his gut told him it might turn into a worst-case scenario. The protestors might do so much damage that he wouldn't have a job to go back to, or the factories might fire all of them and start over—probably with as much automation as possible. His mind drifted towards Marie and flashed a few moments from last night to his conscious thinking, but it didn't last long before it settled on some of her words. She didn't want him to join this movement any more than he had to, but for different reasons. She wanted him to free himself from whatever was holding him back and live his best life possible. He kept thinking about her words: "The factories aren't worth dying for." He had no intention of dying for any cause related to the factories—although he would rather die than grow old in them. He thought she was worried for all the wrong reasons, but in the end agreed with her sentiment; he would not commit to anything that he didn't need to get involved in.

He thought again of the protesters and the tear gas from last night. *Was Jack with them? Was anyone he knew involved in it? They must have been.* The drivers and freight workers were mostly old men, and that mob was moving quickly through the streets. It had to have been a younger crowd to pull off the graffiti and the fire. Would the older men have gone so far as to light the rail cars on fire? Was the entire night just some rebellious students looking for a cause? Whatever the circumstances, Robert decided that his involvement would remain the same: stay united with the workers in terms of working, but don't get involved in taking any action. There was plenty he could do to help people out without throwing any bricks. Always seeing himself as an outsider, Robert decided on his position—he would support them, not *join* them.

The wind pushed the cold through Robert as he walked down the gray street. The sun distanced itself behind the cloud canopy and created the atmosphere of a second morning, even as the day pushed past noon. Everything was a bright, cold gray; the colors of the world took on a subdued sterility as Robert watched them pass by. He approached the only place where anyone would be other than The Bounty. It was a diner walled with windows on a corner a few blocks from his apartment. He saw a few men he recognized from the factories but could tell that none of them would be of any use to him. He was looking for Jack or anyone else that worked on his crew. He pushed on and stopped at a street vendor selling coffee.

"Hey... black coffee." Robert must have stopped here a hundred times in the past two years, but the two men never traded names. The man took up conversation with Robert as he made the drink. "No work today? You men and your strike are killing my business."

"It wasn't up to me. I'd rather be making money to get as far away from here as possible." He wasn't sure this was true, but he knew that in this town, any talk along the lines of being miserable in the factories was received just as easily as talking about the weather.

"Yes... faraway places occupy my mind as well. You're like me; one day this place will be nothing but a terrible memory." He handed Robert his coffee. "I hope so." Robert said as he slid a paper bill across the counter and turned before the man could offer change.

Robert watched the steam of his coffee rise without hesitation as he walked. The wind stopped blowing, the usual buzz of the factories was suppressed, and the bustle of workers usually making their way to subway stations was absent. The day was a cold dead silence, and it filled Robert with unease as The Bounty came into view. The sight of the bar filled him with more unease, as he had never seen it at this time of day. The closest he had come to seeing it in daylight were the few times that he stayed drinking until dawn. But conjuring up those memories stretched his mind to exhaustion. He preferred The Bounty to remain a mystery cloaked in the possibilities of the night. He looked down at the sidewalk to shed the image of The Bounty cast in daylight from his mind as he went for the door.

Inside The Bounty, the smell of stale beer and smoke brought him back to reality. He had floated through town, but now had his feet firm on the ground. He walked towards the bar as his eyes adjusted. When the room came into view, he saw Jack speaking with Frank. Frank was one of the old men of the factory that connected Robert to the past. He liked Frank and was always looking for little signs from him that he had earned his respect. The pair stopped their conversation as soon as they saw Robert approach, and Frank flashed Jack a look of we'll-finish-this-later.

"Robert," Jack said as he pushed an envelope

towards Frank, "grab some food. They've turned this into a regular soup kitchen 'til the strike is over."

Robert looked over and saw a makeshift buffet line set up at one end of the bar. The owner, Larry, was behind the bar. "Yer welcome to anything that's set out there. If you want anything from the kitchen, there's a charge. In fact, anything I serve you at all comes with a charge."

"Now, I thought I was drinking on credit!" Jack mocked as he and Frank abandoned their table for seats at the bar. Robert's stomach turned a little at the sight of the greasy options in their heated trays. His eyes searched until he found something reliable.

The scene in the bar was quiet for the most part. A few of the tables were filled with workers, and the bar was lined with the older men. The old men who had earned their respect were drinking on credit, or probably for free. They had spent their entire lives on those barstools, and they would not let something like money change that.

The tables were filled with a mix of young and old. At one table, young guys were listening intently as the old men spoke as if lecturing them. The young were trading respect for knowledge. Some in other parts of the bar were getting drunk, some were here for the free food, and others showed up simply to hang around because they had nowhere else to go.

"Now, Robert," Frank started, "we're not a union. The unions died generations ago, and we're not going to get into any deliberations with those fuckers in management. But we do look out for each other. It's more of a.... *communal* affair when it comes to these things. Don't jump at the word, we're not gonna march on Washington or anything, we just take care of our own until this thing passes by. You see, Larry here is doing his part with the breakfast, and some…" He looked at Jack. "*Some* are allowed to drink on credit 'til this whole thing blows over. So, we're not asking for *dues* exactly, more of something in the way of donations."

Robert nodded. "Yep, there it is. Why didn't you just search my pockets at the door?"

The look of shock on Frank's face was enough to almost choke Robert on his last bite. He put up a hand to wave it off until he could swallow.

"It was a *joke*, Frank. You know you have my support. I'm not gonna get militant about it and start setting shit on fire, but I'll help out where I can."

Tension froze the bar at the mention of the fire. If the wrong words hit them now, it seemed like they could shatter the men to pieces. "No talk of that fire." Frank looked around. "That was a foolish move. Those actions do not represent us. Some rail workers let those kids from the District in. Those kids don't know a damn thing about working for a living, but they wanna make noise and pretend like they're saving us. What about when summer hits and their mommies and daddies are calling them back to the yacht club? Will they be fighting for us then? I don't wanna hear another goddam word about that fire!" Frank was getting worked up and loud, his face turned red.

"That's fine, Frank, but I'm letting you know. I'm not *organizing*." Robert was speaking loud enough so anyone trying to listen wouldn't have any trouble hearing. Something in him told him he was talking to Jack more than Frank. "I'll help out in terms of survival anyway I can, that's fine, and you know that. It's hard times and we'll get through it together, but that's it. I'm not getting involved in the politics of it all. I'm not gonna be a martyr for someone else's cause. If I wanna die for something, that'll be my decision when the time comes."

"Okay, okay, lower your voice. No one is *organizing*. Now stop talking about it; there's mixed emotions about unions in this room. It's the one argument that could tear us apart. It's better just to not talk about it."

"You're just going to ignore the debate?" Robert's eyes met Frank's, peering at him from behind the pint glass at his mouth.

"God, I hope so. After this is all over, I'm sure a…." he lowered to a whisper, "*organization* will come from it. But that debate is better to take place when we all have income. Right now, we just need to survive this fucking thing."

"Well, where do we stand? What's going on exactly?"

"The strike is unusual. This isn't the normal labor strike over wages or benefits. This is a group of people protesting the fact that they are being replaced by machines. So, the company looks at the strike and says 'so what? These men that are refusing to work are going to be replaced, anyway. They just cut themselves out of the equation a little earlier than we planned.'"

Frank looked around again. People had stopped paying him attention and went back to their own conversations. "The best move we have is to stay in front of the automation, to take labor away from areas that they can't quite replace yet. The drivers won't have any work to come back to; even if they end the strike today, the process is already in place to replace them—they waited too long. Next will be the freight and dock workers. They walked off last night just before the fire. If they stay strong, they can put a hurting on industry. But it's not looking good, industry has a lot of money. They may hold out until labor returns, or they may even speed up the process of automation. The unions, at this point, have no genuine interest in us; if they took up our cause, they would have to dole out strike pay. They see where the future is going too—they won't recoup the strike pay through our union dues by the time the machines take everything from us. If we survive, *then* the unions will move in, but we're on our own for this one." Frank spoke as if he were predicting how a war would be fought.

"Frank, if the entire process is getting automated, what's the point of all this? Why get involved? Instead of the machines pushing us out the door, everyone is just walking out early. The best-case scenario is that we buy ourselves a few months of extra work before it all gets automated. The unions..." he lowered his voice, "... the *unions* are only gonna take up a profitable cause. If there's no people, there's no money in it for them."

"Well, if that's all we got, then that's all we've got. You're young, Robert! You can roam around the world and find another job. There are people here that have given their entire lives to these factories and have nowhere else to go. Their thanks for their lives is to be driven out by some hunk of metal. A machine *we* probably made the parts for! Who knows how many of those machines the drivers transported only to be replaced by them?"

"I feel bad for them, I do. But how is sacrificing everything for something that is inevitable going to do anything but cause trouble for me? I'm all for charity, I am, but am I supposed to dedicate my life to this thing?"

"Well, *you* don't have much to worry about. You run and fix the machines. You won't be replaced anytime soon, but when you are, you'll wish you'd done something about it today!" He was getting red again.

"Frank, calm down. I told you I would help, but there has to be some sort of goal to work towards. We can't call for all of industry to stop utilizing machines that will save them millions each year. You know that's not going to happen. We can't tell them to keep our jobs just for the sake of us. You know they don't care. We can resist all we want, but what's the point? What are your demands to a company, a whole industry even, that can go on without you?"

"The only thing left is severance pay and pension," Frank said with a defeated look into his beer. "We want a contract that guarantees livable pay once the machines come in, and we'll promise a smooth transition into automation. For younger guys like you, we want cross-training to maintain the machines."

"It seems like a long shot. No one is going to pay you for nothing. Jobs to maintain the machines will present themselves as a need arises. You know that—there's no point in demanding something that is going to happen, anyway."

"Robert, you're smarter than most guys here. You can see where this is going, but a lot of guys here have nothing. They can't accept the changes that are coming to the world. They believe there is something to be gained from this, and we need to keep them thinking that for their full involvement. Don't go around trying to enlighten people, just show your support."

"That's fine, Frank. That's not a problem, I will support people who are out of work—that part we're all in together, but don't look to me to take an active role in saving *positions*. I'm not part of a *cause*."

"Alright, Alright, Robert. If I were young, I would probably do the same. But take a look around this bar; no one is gonna hire a bunch of old men like this just so they can retire in what? Three or five years? Nobody. Think of this as our form of bingo night; we don't have jobs and we need something to do—one last fight. I see your point, but you gotta respect mine. I'm giving these guys something to live for right now, and there's still a chance, a *chance* that we might actually get something from it."

Robert nodded, and they both calmed down. Frank finished his beer and placed it on the bar. Robert reached into his pocket and laid a few bills down, as he signaled the bartender for two more.

"Next one's on me, for the greater good." Robert joked, but behind his words, he was taking a risk. He watched Frank's face carefully for a reaction.

A smile broke Frank's face. "Oh, Robert the humanitarian!" He turned to Jack, who was already laughing.

"Oh, it doesn't stop there." Robert produced a pack of Marie's cigarettes, took one for himself and offered the pack up to Frank and Jack, who each withdrew one.

"Did you switch brands?" Jack knew him best.

Robert experienced a slight panic. He didn't want to think about defining what he and Marie had between them. He also didn't want to subject her to the vulgar opinions of The Bounty, even if she wasn't there to hear them. "I just take what I can get. These are hard times, remember?" Robert started his cigarette and let out a long exhale.

Before Jack had a chance to interrogate him any further, The Bounty brightened with a flash of the front door opening and the sound of excitement. One of the factory workers burst through the door with a piece of paper that looked like an eviction notice. He shouted to the room, "It's a lockout! They fuckin' locked us out!"

Cheers and hollers were heard from around the room. The man looked confused and took the paper to one of the elders sitting at a table near the wall. Robert brought his attention back to Frank. "Why the hell is everyone so happy? Now we can't go back to work even if we wanted to."

"Exactly! We just went from un*willing* to work, to un*able* to work! We can all draw unemployment! They must have thought it was a power move, but they just gave us funding!" Frank let out a laugh.

Jack leaned across the bar towards Robert while patting Frank on the back. "Well, alright, old man. If you can pay for your own drinks, then our work here is done. Me and Robert will go scout out the factories and see what the scene is down there."

"If you make it around to the Department of Labor, bring me back the forms. I'm not waiting in line. If they've run out, I'll just give it a few days. Either way, come back and let me know what's going on out there."

"You got it," said Jack as he turned to leave.

Robert stood, slid his fresh beer towards Frank, and said nothing as he extended his hand out to shake. He cared more about respect from the old man than anything to do with labor politics. Frank accepted the offering and shook his hand. Robert walked away with confidence. He knew where he stood with the men and with himself.

4

Robert and Jack exited The Bounty and stepped into the bright, gray light of the street. Jack turned his head down until his eyes adjusted. "I never expect daylight when I go through that door. What do you say we go the long way to our jobs and see if there is any action? I don't really expect there would be just yet. That lock out is an early move..." Jack looked down the street in thought. The lock-out was a sudden move, almost as if it were planned before the strike happened.

Robert looked down the street, and they both began walking as he spoke to the air. "You'd think we were in the midst of a revolution. It sure excites you."

"It does. It's a movement. These guys would rather see the factories burn than be overrun by machines and computers. I wouldn't mind too much, myself. I hate this fuckin' place. How'd you know about the fire already?"

"I was there."

"Don't try convincing me you had anything to do with it, not after all that shit you told Frank."

"No, with a girl from the District. We went out there last night, just to get away from everything and breathe a little."

"Lucy?"

An unexpected shock ran through Robert. His emotions attached to Lucy were fading further from his mind, but he wasn't expecting to have her thrust right back into it so soon. "No, one of her roommates. The Lucy thing was going nowhere."

"I could've told you that months ago. You're not the first guy she's strung along."

Robert turned to look at Jack. "*You?*"

"She tried, but I'd seen her do it to enough guys by that time. I gave up on it much earlier than you did. How long have you been goin' around with her roommate?"

Blood rushed to Robert's ears. He then turned around and walked backwards to face Jack. "You don't need to worry about it."

"Yeah, yeah." Jack smirked as he shoved one of Robert's shoulders to spin him back around. The two continued towards the factories, turning the corner leading down the street to the main office of their branch. Although everyone looked at the industrial zone as one entity, it comprised at least a few dozen different companies that all worked together. The offices for all the companies were in one sector. This way, the executives from the companies only saw each other and never had to deal with any of the workers.

Jack shimmied a newspaper out of a machine on their route. It was from two days prior. "I guess everyone is out of work. Can't even get a newspaper," Jack said as he held it up for Robert to see. The major headline, in bold letters, read: "Strike?"

Jack folded up the newspaper and threw it in a trash can. He looked at Robert to see if the headline stirred up anything, but Robert's mind was somewhere else. He was trying to find a sense of direction as they penetrated the industrial zone and came up on the recruiting sector.

The front of industry, entered at any angle other than the sea, was a jungle of propaganda made to look promising for any potential investors or employees. The floor-to-ceiling windows of the lobbies were adorned with pictures and posters of people smiling. They depicted sparkling clean machines and gleaming towers of inventory. Robert put his head up to a window with his hands over his eyes to cut the glare. His eyes were greeted with info-graphs of numbers that meant nothing to them now—safety, production, sales. There were pictures of models dressed up as factory workers with quotes about the great working conditions. The abandoned streets of propaganda sent dystopian chills through Robert as they made their way to the offices. Newspapers and leaves rustled past them as if to punctuate the desolation.

"Not much action here," Robert said to the abandoned corridor.

"I didn't think there would be, probably nothin' on the next few blocks either. I don't expect we'll see anyone until we make it to the factories. We're only two days in, though. They probably don't even have a picket line set up. That lockout move really changed how this is gonna play out."

"Yeah," Robert let out softly as he kept looking in the windows from the street.

"What's wrong with you? You act like you've never seen this place. Didn't you get hired in through here?"

"No, I did it over the phone. Then I went straight to test at the Department of Labor. After that, they gave me a factory address to report to." Robert still seemed distant as he looked from one side of the street to another.

"Right, this wasn't your first factory gig. I forgot you jumped straight in with us. Well, you missed out on a free lunch and a few cups of coffee. But at least you didn't show up to work and realize you had been lied to. I've seen the look on a new guy's face when reality sets in; takes about a week or two and then we never see 'em again."

"I knew what I was getting into." Robert didn't like being tossed in with the *new guys*. He didn't care how long he had been working at a job. He had worked in factories since his first job; there was nothing new about it to him. Even after a few years, Jack and the other men saw him as the new guy. He might have been new to their factory, but he wasn't new to the work. He let himself get frustrated and took out his cigarettes. It was the last pack of the three that he bought with Marie. Depression tugged at him when he saw they were almost gone. But as he smoked, the flavor sent warmth and memories of his time with Marie through him. He paid little attention to Jack or his surroundings. He smoked and thought of Marie, conjuring her spirit and embracing the warmth that she gave him.

Jack and Robert pushed through the maze of propaganda. "Since you've never been here, you may not have noticed the lack of subway stations. No bus stops either. The closest ones are a decent walk from here. That way, when people are done with their business, they can't go exploring where the rich people are. They might think about it, but they gotta keep in mind the long walk to add on top of any exploring. It's designed to keep us out." Jack watched Robert absorb his words. He hoped the design of the city would reveal the design of society, of their fates.

They turned right and looked up at the massive buildings that lined the streets. They had reached the main drag that ran straight through all of industry and eventually opened to the sea. Robert looked up at the buildings. He was physically and mentally dwarfed by their intensity. The authority of the Brutalist structures pushed down on his chest.

"Aaah, the financial sector, home of the elite," Jack let out as he opened his arms to the street. The mammoth buildings streamed down from the sky and drove themselves straight into the bedrock. Looking up at their height made Robert dizzy. He was sure he could sense the rotation of the planet in their presence. He saw his place in the universe and knew he was miniscule.

"Do they really need to be this big?" Robert asked in awe.

"They gotta keep that money somewhere," Jack half-joked. "It's all designed for show, like everything else in this place. All the gigantic buildings only line this street. Look down the streets connecting: a skyscraper, neighbors a café and courtyard. The main corridor is all business and intimidation to put on a show for the outsiders. The side streets jutting out are all luxury and leisure for the bigwigs."

Robert looked down a side street and saw a two-story café sharing a wall with a skyscraper. Not a single building down the side street was over twenty feet in height. It reminded him of the fake movie town in an old Western he had seen. He half expected to see actors playing roles to give the street life, but there was no one. Although the street lay deserted, it still vibrated with energy. Instead of desolation, there was the energy of life, as if a crowd were present just a moment earlier. He wondered if the rich designed the buildings to emanate a live sense of anticipation in their absence.

Robert scanned the skyscrapers one last time before returning his attention to Jack. "This is ridiculous. You guys run your operation out of a dive bar. You think you can compete with all this?"

"They're nothing without the workers. They think they can replace everyone with machines? They're wrong. This isn't the only industrial town around. The whole country is made up of places like this. You've seen it, you've come from it." Jack was gearing up for a debate and began his assault. "The Bounty only plays a small role in it. We're the guys that don't have families and are crazy enough to live here. There are a hundred bars like that throughout the suburbs, thousands across the state, with thousands of people in them talking about what we're talking about. And there're more workers at home supporting their families who are on the brink of losing everything. What do they think is gonna happen when they've got an army of people with nothing more to lose, focusing their rage on them? You think they can hide in these buildings? There's nothing in there but desks and paper. They can't live on bureaucracy and architecture. It's work that creates life."

Robert shook his head. "You really let Frank get in your head. This isn't a nationwide crisis, Jack! This is a few old men in a bar losing their jobs, and you want to lead a fuckin' revolution over it. Even if it was a nationwide crisis, what do you think we're gonna accomplish here? If the *whole* country is out of work, then we're fucked, even if we do save this town! If you think the world is changing, then adjust your life to deal with it! You think setting a few train cars on fire is gonna change the world?!"

"Yes! I do! What we do here, other people will do everywhere else. But if we don't do it, then how can we expect anyone else will? At least I'm doing something about it! You think drinking wine with those art-school girls in their beloved District is gonna make any difference in *your* life? Once the novelty of spending time with a broke factory worker has worn off, you're gonna be left alone with nothing but those old men in the bar to fall back on." Jack was calmer than Robert thought he would be, but he knew he had been waiting for this argument—it had probably been well rehearsed.

Robert confirmed his suspicions. "I knew someone familiar was in that mob. You still smell like smoke. You hate the District scene so much, but you sure seemed pretty deep with them last night."

Jack rejected the thought. "They're good for something. At least they're willing to participate in something! I'd rather manipulate *them* than have it the other way around. How is Lucy anyway?"

It was a cheap shot, but still sent a dagger of jealousy through Robert's chest. They were standing in the middle of an intersection. Robert backed up and thought about whether he was going to fight Jack right there in the middle of the street. He stood tense and looked Jack in his eye. It was a personal shot, but that meant Jack knew he was losing the argument. He didn't want to fight Jack—he didn't want to lose him as a friend — but he was still angry with him.

He thought about retaliating with something just as personal, but then decided against it. As he watched Jack, he let the anger flow through his body.

The Brutalist buildings stood like an eager crowd watching Jack and Robert. The air stood still. The dead leaves seemed like they flattened out and stuck to the ground as if to avoid the argument. A silence insulated by the buildings took over. Robert calmed; the anger slowly drained from his body into the asphalt. He stood numb and empty as he held off letting another demeanor take over.

Robert then broke the moment. "Alright. I'm done with this. You're delusional, Jack. I don't want to hear any more about your theories on society. I agree with you on most of this, I really do. I see the rich and their designs against the poor. I see the conspiracies in all of it. But agreeing with you ends with what you think we should do about it. I just show up to work, do my job, and take the money to go live my life. I can see the design of the system every day, but I don't see myself as a part of it; that's where we're different. I don't care what the rich do, it has no effect on how I manage my life. I don't care if the entire world gets overrun by machines; I'll be more than happy to never have to show up at a factory again. I'll find something else to do. The whole world can lose their jobs, and I'll find something else to do. I live my life in the world I find myself in, and I change as the world changes. A few days ago, we had to work for a living. Now we have to help each other out and collect unemployment to get by; so, I make the change and keep living my life. How hard is that? The world is out of our control. Instead of trying to change the world, you could focus all that energy on figuring out how to navigate through it. Do you have any idea how much of the world you would have to change for guys like us to succeed? We have a better chance changing how we interact with it if we want anything to get better for ourselves."

Jack absorbed every word but had no response other than to stand still with thought. Robert gave him enough time to let it sink in and then walked away as Jack watched him. When enough distance extended between them, Jack started walking again. The two kept a few dozen feet apart as they walked through the rest of the financial sector—two lone signs of life meandering through an apocalyptic city on the edge of industry; they were in complete disagreement with each other but reliant on each other at the same time. After a few blocks, the buildings around them came to an abrupt halt, revealing a bridge that seemed to push apart the land of the rich from the land of the workers. One after the other, they drifted onto the bridge. The buildings shrank in the skyline behind their shoulders as if they were no longer trying to impress with their size and wealth. Halfway across, Robert looked back to see that Jack was still behind him; the wind's sharp chill from the water made the bridge seem longer than it was. With the false drags of time, Robert slowed his pace as he was nearing the opposite end of the bridge and let Jack catch up. The time alone was good for their demeanors.

Jack was the first to speak as he met Robert where the bridge touched land. As they stopped, Jack leaned against the railing that led down to the trains. "No signs of life here, either. I didn't think there would be. The next few blocks are all for lower management and paper pushing, then it's a few miles of other factories before ours. You wanna catch a train to our jobs?"

Robert was starting the last two of Marie's cigarettes. He inhaled both, returned the lighter to his back pocket, and then gave one to Jack. He exhaled over Jack's head and then over towards the offices. "Might as well. It's a long walk, and even if we run into anyone out here, it won't make a difference. The trains are running. I heard them under the bridge."

They walked down the stairs to the turnstiles. Robert patted his pocket and smirked as he realized Marie had his metro card. He went over to the kiosk and bought a day pass, secretly smiling to himself the entire time. Jack was already on the other side, waiting for him. They met up and walked around a tiled curve that led to the platform where a train was already waiting. They flicked their butts into the gap between the train and platform before entering the empty car and taking seats on either side. As if the train sensed them, the doors closed, and it began to move.

Nothing was said between Jack and Robert.

Nothing else could be said. They knew where each other stood, and neither was going to change. They were out on an errand together, and how the other one felt about it didn't matter. Jack laid across the seats, looking at the advertisements angled down at him from the ceiling. Robert was scanning a two-day-old paper; a dozen copies were scattered across the seats. They remained in silence until they exited the train at their stop, where they were surprised to see the newspaper stand was open.

"That's a small miracle. We were out of smokes." Robert said, trailing Jack as they made their approach.

The stand was an octagon of heavily shellacked wood in the center of a tile and concrete plaza. The open end faced the path between the trains and the stairs. The metal gate was up, and the magazine racks were set out, but the shelves where the newspapers were usually held were as barren as the streets above. The attendant within seemed impartial to their arrival.

"Hey, let me get a pack of smokes." Jack pushed a bill across the counter. "You see anyone out here today?"

"No, a few stragglers here and there—it's been a slow day. What brings you guys out here?"

"Just checkin' out our jobs to see if anything's goin' on—seeing if we can gather any info for the old men."

"Not much goin' on here, but I get paid by the

hour. You guys want any of this coffee? I'm just gonna toss it, anyway. No one's gonna buy it." Before they had a chance to respond, he was already pouring two cups of burnt coffee. Jack took his coffee and cigarettes and made his way up the stairs as Robert went to the window and got three more packs of Marie's brand of cigarettes. He paid the attendant and raised his cup in thanks, and then caught up with Jack.

At the top of the stairs, they placed their coffees atop a covered trash can; Jack tore open his cigarettes and went right to smoking as Robert tucked two packs into his back pockets and then began packing the last one against his hand before opening the pack, throwing away the wrapper, and starting his cigarette. He made eye contact with Jack through the entire routine with sarcasm, as if to intimidate him with his ritual. With the cigarette in his lips, he picked up both coffees and gave one to Jack.

The two stood in tight hoodies and stiff work pants with their boots firmly planted on the ground. The cold air gently played with the steam and smoke dancing away from their hands. The movement mimicked the smoke and steam, leaving the stacks that jutted towards the sky. The factories were so tightly built together that they looked like they were leaning over the two interlopers, inspecting them as a nuisance. The two stood in silence and returned the glare of the callous, Brutalist empire. They stood tall as the buildings across the street seemed to lean in closer, threatening to snuff them out. The steam from the sewers was all that stood between them. As tensions rose, it came to life as a ghostly apparition pacing the middle of the street, mimicking a referee with his arms out, keeping fighters apart before a boxing match. Jack and Robert smoked and drank their coffee, unwavering and unwilling to give up any ground. They knew these buildings; they knew their torment. This piece of earth was where man and machine had merged as one.

The wind picked up and pushed down over the factories; smoke and steam curled down, becoming great claws ready to pounce on their prey. The two stood as the steam danced around them and teased them, as if trying to get them to make the first move. Another wild current of wind curled up the face of the factories, creating a tidal wave of thick steam and smoke that swelled up into the sky and blocked out the sun. Streetlights flickered on as wind howled through the streets and streams of vapor thrashed down on Jack and Robert. Phantom arms and claws curled up and cracked down through the artificial dusk like bullwhips, cracking the asphalt in a display of metaphysical intimidation, but the two stood unprovoked, waiting for the next move. With the vibrating energy of each crack, blood pumped through and fortified their muscles to prepare for a physical assault, yet the two stood calm. They had a psychic connection with the factories, as if they were all siblings who had experienced the same childhood trauma together. Jack and Robert watched the factories lash out the same way two older brothers would watch a younger one throw a tantrum over a hardship of their upbringing they knew too well. Jack and Robert knew nothing could be done to comfort the child, other than to let the tantrum run its course. They knew what the machines and factories were going through; they knew it would pass, and they knew that they would have to remain until the end to project affection and console their mystic comrade.

Under the scrutiny of the factories, Jack and Robert were recognized as what they were, neither adversaries nor prey, but equals. The factories could break men but also need the empathy of man to flourish. Each hated the other to the extent that they represented to each other the circumstances in which they found themselves, yet they depended on each other to share their existence. They shared torment as men wrangled machines and factories into submission. Man, machine, and the factories that detain them reject each other while justifying each other's existence. It made no difference what compelled them, whether it was socialism, capitalism, or even charity. Machine and man faced off, even though it was the process they rejected more than each other. They found themselves enslaved against their will, resenting each other but needing each other. The workers that occupy these factories were born into the working class against their will; snatched from the ethereal bosom of the natural and spiritual intentions of the universe to be forced and formed by a deteriorated form of a society that was birthed from savages as an aspiration of enlightenment. The worker's soul, *raw ether*, is slingshot through the universe with a trajectory towards spiritual infinity and then manifested as a human in an alienated reality where it is expected in a brief physical lifetime to make sense of an existence and civilization that no known natural entity was meant to endure. With few choices other than poverty or death, stuck in the middle of the raging currents of competition, humans must concede, consciously or not, to abandon the origins and potentials of their souls and let the manufacturing world deteriorate their hopes, dreams, and desires into conformed standards and outlooks so that they may fit into the slots of the working class. Just the same, the factories' raw makeup was torn from the Earth and forced and formed into a sterile derivative of society's misguided aspirations. The machines are forged in the furnaces of greed and corruption in the name of innovation and forced into the factories like compressed springs, screaming for rest yet vibrating with energy. Built not only to house machine and man but to integrate with their functions, the factories are cursed to stand as monuments to failure, with their only hope being that the eternal passing of time would magnanimously erode them back into the earth. Both the inanimate and the human entities: sweating, steaming, screaming, and bleeding as their wills cry out in torment to produce for the gain of another. To work for the rich is to die of soul-asphyxiation—to die in the mental torments of what has become reality so that the few can experience faux paradise.

Jack and Robert made inventory of their psychic connection with the factories as their minds came back to the street. At the height of its intensity, the storm on the street reversed with a sudden vacuum of energy. As the wind stopped and fell flat, the smoke and steam fell with it, evaporating on contact with the asphalt. The buildings stood erect; their smokestacks stood lifeless, backlit by the white sky, with a diffused sun radiating through it. The coffee and cigarettes produced no fumes. The world stood still for a few moments in the deafening silence. Slowly, as the streetlights flickered out of existence, the hum of the factories could be heard again, and the smog calmly wafted from the towers to the clouds. Robert blew the steam from his coffee and drank, then folded its taste with that of the cigarette's smoke. His tongue tingled as he exhaled and looked over at Jack. They made deliberate eye contact and without words knew that their earlier argument was over and that they were united as one force. Jack leaned back on the handrail by the stairs, took a long final drag off his cigarette, flicked its butt towards the factories as if to brush off the episode, and took stride next to Robert as they crossed the bullwhipped cracks on the street and entered their factory.

Jack and Robert sensed something was out of place as they entered the factory. The industrial smells and sounds that usually anchored their senses gave way to charged stimuli. The pungent odor of industry had diffused into the sour smell of sweat and humanity, while the droning motors and cycling processes were replaced by an irregular rhythm of clinks and clangs echoing through the concrete chamber. Their firm sense of unity with the factories weakened as they penetrated deeper. As their eyes adjusted, a manifestation obstructed what should have been the familiar sight of their workstations. Rows of tall glistening robotics, still braced in wood frames and shipping plastic, appeared before them and extended back towards the far end of the factory, where they faded in the dust and darkness. The mechanized terra-cotta army stood as if poised to usher in the new automated age of industry from some spiritual realm.

Nothing could be said between Jack and Robert—their journey from The Bounty had put them on the same wavelength. Knowing what the other was thinking, the pair stood and absorbed the scene before them as it revealed to them their fates and consequences. The past two days had put their futures in jeopardy, but they didn't expect the change to be so sudden or to show up in such force. Until now, it seemed like the future could somehow be reversed or that they would have enough time to adjust to the new set of circumstances that lay ahead for them. As they stood under the scrutiny of a new era, they came to understand that no matter how much energy they put into constructing comfortable mental states or perfect moments, they couldn't live in them forever. Automation replacing their jobs made them realize they were being thrust through their lives without the luxury of resting in comfortable moments. If they wanted any ease in this life, they would have to move faster than their circumstances.

A sudden rush of sound broke Jack and Robert from their spell. They followed it to the source, where they could have guessed they were going to find Lou in a panic. They had a small sense of comfort at the sight of him, but it was shattered as they saw him talking to a group of workers that didn't belong in their factory. With a few terse instructions, the men dispersed, leaving Lou out in the open as Jack and Robert closed in.

Jack pounced. "Who are those guys?"

"Ah..." Lou fumbled over his next few words as he looked in the direction of the men and then back at Jack and Robert. He almost seemed embarrassed at being caught. His appearance didn't help establish any confidence with Jack or Robert—he was greasy and tired. As he spoke, his gestures rattled under strain; his nerves were racked by caffeine. "While everything is down, the equipment is being upgraded. You know nothing ever gets done while the machines are in production."

Jack was beside himself. "Come on, Lou! You really think we don't know what automation looks like?" He stared Lou down as his chest tensed and his throat began choking him. With no response from Lou, he looked to Robert for some sort of comradery. Instead of chiming in, Robert braced himself with a deep breath and could respond with nothing other than to return a glare into Jack's raging eyes. Jack clenched his jaw with anger and took a deep breath. "I've seen what I came for. I'll be at The Bounty." He turned and left Robert and Lou together as he threaded his way through the new machinery.

Lou saw his chance to appeal to Robert. "How do you run these things?! We need numbers, any numbers! I don't care if I get one finished product off this line today. I need something to report!"

The words brought Robert back to reality. "What are you talking about? Everything is at a standstill."

"I just need the machines to run!" Lou flustered.

"Lou, there's no material coming in. How can you run the machines if you've got nothing to feed them? And what difference does it make? It looks like this place will crank out plenty of inventory without us once these things come to life."

Lou uttered a very stern "Robert," signifying there was no debating the automation before returning to the present crisis. "They don't care! My bosses need numbers! They don't care about the details, all that matters is production! I need something to report!"

"Lou, what the hell is wrong with you? The situation is completely out of your hands. How can you stress out about something that you have no control over? I would think this would be the calmest point of your life. Tell them exactly what you see in this factory straight down to the piers. They should be able to do the math. No people equals no work."

"You guys don't know what it's like! I don't get to come in every day and just fuck around with the machines until it's time to go. If the machines break, you don't care, you just go drink a pot of coffee with a pack of smokes. Hell, most of you probably look forward to machine downtime, but I'm responsible! I'm LIABLE! I have to have numbers!"

Lou's face was red and pouring sweat. His hair was a shamble and yellowed sweat stains blotted his shirt. It was clear to Robert through his appearance that he hadn't slept for days. As Robert was making his visual assessment, Lou tried one last appeal.

"Robert, please! Get this thing running!"

Lou looked like a madman. His words dropped in front of Robert as if a stray piece of the ceiling had fallen between them. Robert backed up with a slight sense of alarm, thinking Jack and his scrutiny may be lurking somewhere nearby. The sure fact that he would report everything that had happened in the next few moments to Frank prompted him to choose his words carefully. He fortified his stance to help his fellow factory workers without getting too involved politically.

"Lou, you know I can't. I'm with the rest of the guys on this one. I can't work for you while all this is going on."

"Robert, there aren't any unions! Don't listen to any of that shit you hear at The Bounty! I'll pay you; I'll pay you with my own money. Even with payroll shut down, I can still give you cash. We just need numbers!"

"Lou, it's not just about the guys, it's just not practical. There's nothing to feed the machines with, there's no raw material coming from the ports. I was at the piers last night; the ships are backed out to the horizon. Hell, there's nowhere to even store inventory with our replacements taking up all the free space!" Robert was exasperated. His cheeks burned, and his mind was going into overdrive.

"I don't care if we have to tear down the walls or dismantle the goddam machines to feed them to themselves! Just show me, I'll run it myself!" Lou took off towards Robert's usual machine, yelling something about the controls. Robert trailed behind and watched as Lou continued ranting and jerked at the controls, but his misgivings were ignored.

"Lou," Robert called for his attention, but the man was still on a rant about the machines and production.

"LOU!" Robert yelled at the man with a tone that cut through the sweat and grease and turned his brain stem to ice. Lou momentarily sobered up out of his delirium and turned around to face Robert.

"What is all this? How are they automating us already? I thought it was just distribution."

Lou ran up to Robert while waving his hands in dismissal. "That's nothing. That's nothing you were meant to see. Don't worry about it."

The rage of disloyalty building within Robert.

"Lou, you've got me working late in here. You've got me putting off things in my life as if I'm supposed to be a loyal worker." He thought of his missed opportunities with Lucy, but he acted as if the whole potential of his life was slipping from his grasp. His throat raged with so much fiery blood that his words caught fire as they thrust towards Lou. "You owe me this!" Robert was close to shouting or choking. He didn't know which. "What is this? How long did you know they were automating everything? Is this what I get for working for you? You don't even give any of us the decency of telling us it might be time to start looking for new jobs when you saw this coming?!"

Lou was desperately trying to slide back into his delirium as a defense mechanism. He did not want to confront the reality of the situation with Robert. He wanted nothing to do with this conversation. "Nothing is changing, Robert. You know you're going into maintenance!"

"Try telling Jack he has to work on machines that are meant to replace everyone he looks up to!" Robert was falling into Lou's delirium.

"Don't pay any attention to Jack! He tries to romanticize every aspect of these factories and turn every mundane daily task into a philosophy. He'll do the work!" Lou gestured towards the machines. "Whether or not he can relate it to the meaning of the universe, someone needs to keep those god-forsaken things running. I've got you guys set up. You're not going to lose your jobs to automation, you're going to transition."

"What about the other guys? You think I can come here and look those guys in the eye as I work on a machine that's meant to send them out the door? You're not giving me a choice; you're pinning me against them in this thing. You know I actually have to go out in the real world and interact with them! You've got it all figured out for us in here, but what are we supposed to do when we step outside those doors and deal with those men in the real world?"

Lou looked like a frustrated father dealing with a child that couldn't grasp one of his life lessons. "It's just *work*, Robert. It's just a *job*—this has nothing to do with life. Those old men believe in their old-school ideals, but the world doesn't work like that anymore. Hell, it never even worked that way to begin with. They're just using guys like Jack in their fight for a pension. You think *I'm* not including you in the plans? Do you really think those guys plan on taking care of you once they get what they want out of all this?"

It was too much. Robert's faculties were fluctuating between overdrive and melt-down. His neurons were erratic. He was overwhelmed and did not know how his mind was going to begin to settle on a position towards all of this. He looked over in the direction that Jack took off in. He focused on the crates of machines, then finally back on Lou, who somehow knew what Robert was experiencing.

"Don't look into it too much." Lou looked at Robert and for a split second almost felt something like empathy before his attention ran back to where it was when they found him. He looked back at the machine and thought of his numbers. "Please get this going! I just need to figure it out. I need to make a production report!" He ran back to the controls but couldn't get it to run. With Lou's moment of humanity over, Robert took the opportunity to leave before Lou noticed. He could hear more clanging and shouting at the machine as he made his way through the door. He thought he would find Jack on the other side, but it was just an empty, cold, gray street.

5

Later that night, Robert found himself in a familiar stance, looking up at the doorway to Lucy and Marie's house. Minus the one he was smoking. His pockets were tight with her brand of cigarettes. In his other hand, he held what was left of the bottle of vodka she had brought over the night before. Between drags of smoke, he patted his pockets down, comforting himself by taking inventory. He stood with his work boots firmly planted on the concrete. He contemplated how different his state of mind was compared to the last time he was here. He was aware of the scrutiny of the always watching sea of molten clouds churning in the heavens above him, as if to keep score as his fate unfolded. In the short time since he last stood here, his position in life, his relation to the world around him, and his place in the universe had changed. He wasn't sure what to think as he took a final drag and walked up the steps, but he took comfort that this time there was no desperation. There was no hope or uncertainty as he approached the door; he knew Marie was expecting him, yet his nerves still stiffened as he raised his hand to knock.

His nerves thawed at the last moment, and as his fist came down to knock at the door, it dropped and went for the knob instead. He opened and entered the door to find Marie in the kitchen, where she was emptying the contents of two water bottles into the sink.

"Robert!" She turned and hugged him with her hands filled. He returned the embrace with one hand placed between her shoulder blades.

He looked at the bottles. "Should I even ask what you're up to?"

She half smiled with mischievous eyes. "Always," she said, and she liberated the vodka from his grasp. Robert sat at the island as he watched her fill the water bottles with vodka.

"Vodka to go? This should be an interesting evening."

After the bottles were filled, Marie took a shot of what remained of the vodka. She grimaced and slid the bottle towards Robert. "Well, we're not going out to the piers. There may actually be people on the train. I thought we could go see what everyone is up to out in the woods tonight."

There was a weakness in his chest, but he couldn't let the reaction take hold; it took everything to keep the burn of the vodka in his throat tamed. He wasn't in a drinking mood, but he was almost thankful that the burn was there so that she couldn't see his emotion. He was familiar with it and wasted no time exploring it. He was looking forward to a domestic night alone with Marie. All he desired most at this moment was to be alone with someone and find complete comfort in them. Once again, he faced having to share someone's attention with the rest of the world.

Sensing his disappointment, she said, "We can just stay for the night and be gone in the morning. We can be all alone in this great big house as much as you like until they come back."

He couldn't take more disappointment or any sort of negativity in his mind. He had no energy left for it. He eyed the contents of the bottle, took a measured shot of exactly half and slid the bottle back to Marie. "If we must." She returned his smile and excitedly finished off the vodka. "Come with me," she said, and she took off, gliding up the stairs.

The sudden introduction of alcohol into his bloodstream had him wondering whether she was a woman or a spirit as he conceded and followed her up the stairs, and by the time he reached her room, he had reached an equilibrium of comfort. He sat on her bed and watched her pack a bag. He moved to the end of the bed near the window, started a cigarette, and let the warm air of the room carry the smoke out into the night.

He thought it was strange to be so comfortable in Lucy's house. Even without her being present he expected her energy to penetrate him. He looked around the room at the moving boxes and wondered whether she was packing or if she had just never fully unpacked. The art school students came and went so frequently and got so wrapped up in their projects that it could be either. He didn't commit too much thought to it because he knew Marie was the type of person who couldn't be anchored down. She would leave boxes half unpacked just to express that she hadn't fully committed to a place.

He crawled out the window and sat on the roof. He wondered at the sky as it looked down on him—wondered how much of it was natural. How much of the steam and smoke from the factories was up there joining with the veritable clouds? Or was it all pollution? He decided it was probably all pollution, mostly chemicals suspended in steam. As he thought of the factories, he became apprehensive. Before he could explore the meaning in full, he heard Marie coming through the window and joining him by his side.

"Hey... that jawline is pretty tight, you ok?"

"Yeah, just tired. It was a long day."

"Mmmh, are you not feeling social this evening?"

"No, not at all." He let out a sigh. "We can still go, but I don't want you to feel like you're dragging me around if I'm not in the mood. Can we just sit awhile? Give me a little time out here with you and I'll be good enough to go anywhere." He was expecting a warm response, or even a smile, but she matched his tone and started a cigarette in response as she leaned against him. "You got it."

They both sat in silence, looking up at the

sky. There wasn't much to awe at, but it was enough to keep them occupied. The magma-colored clouds slowly swirled and moved away from them. It was an illusion that would continually repeat itself. It was constantly moving, yet always looked the same. It reminded Robert of the surface of the sun.

Robert had a stray thought. "Do you think it ever snows here?"

"Chernobyl style fall-out snow or actual snow?" She looked over at him but received no response other than his disconnected gaze towards the sky. "No..." She carefully maneuvered around whatever mood he might be in. "No, I don't think the factories will allow it. It gets cold, but I think besides all the steam, all the heat from the factories would melt it all before it got to us."

He remained looking up and out. Marie finished her cigarette and flicked it into a gutter. She then rolled on her hip in order to straddle Robert and put her face in his line of vision.

"What is with you? What did you do today that turned you into a statue?"

Robert's exterior flaked as he looked into her playful eyes. "I went to check in at The Bounty and meet up with Jack, then we went down to check out the scene at our jobs."

She rolled her eyes at the end of his sentence. "Well, no reason you're in such a stoic mood. You're finally on leave from the factories and you decide to go to them, anyway? What do you gain by visiting an empty factory?" she asked with a slight laugh.

He inhaled hard. "That's the problem. They were full. Full of automated machines to replace everyone. Full of what could only have been the workers from all those ships who have no problem coming ashore to install the machines for extra cash. It's all coming faster than anyone could think."

"I thought you didn't want to get involved in any of this. You were just going to help out with the guys and then figure something out. Those factories have nothing to do with you."

"The factories are easy. When I go to work, I have nothing to worry about, I leave the outside world outside and I lose myself in the work. Now…"

"Now you have to face reality?"

Robert didn't want to agree. He remained silent and tried to look away, but she was taking up his entire field of vision. He reached for a cigarette as a distraction. But instead of getting away from her, he made the mistake of starting two and including her in his distraction. She was able to dig deeper.

"You know you're better than those factories. You know you're better than everyone who's going to spend a lifetime in them. I don't know what kind of rut you're in, but avoiding your life by working it away is not an answer. This conflict is a good thing; you *should* think about your life. How it has been up to this point and where it's going. Did you think you could just avoid participating in your own life?"

Robert let his protective layers melt away and decided to honestly answer her question.

"Well, yeah. I mean, I haven't thought about it." He smiled at the absurdity. "I guess I avoided thinking about that, too. It's just, it worked. If you go to work, people just assume you're being responsible, they assume you're taking care of it all." He squeezed his hands wherever they were on her body to let her know he was thinking. She held her thoughts and waited for the rest of it. "When you work all the time, no one asks questions, and no one forces you to answer them. People see work as an unavoidable part of life, and if you throw yourself at it..." He paused to cement his notion. "When you work, people leave you alone. Work is a socially excusable absence from participating in life—you can even leave yourself alone while you go through the motions." He was beginning to tremble with honesty. It was the first time in a long time that he let someone know exactly how he felt at the present moment.

Her hands caressed his chest as she proceeded with caution. "You work to avoid facing your own life, but if you do it long enough, it's no longer a choice. You become your work and get stuck in those factories like everyone else." She tried to ease up a little and not sound like she was lecturing him. "Just because things are changing doesn't mean you have to face all of life's questions at once. Things *are* changing, but they haven't changed yet. Accepting that is a big part of facing life, just knowing and being able to prepare yourself."

He breathed deep, "But it was so easy. As long as I was going through the motions, I didn't have to answer, or even *ask*, 'What am I going to do with my life?'"

She laughed like a mother looking down at a child that was worried about something that only grown-ups worry about. "You can't beat yourself up for not knowing something that most people live their whole lives without figuring out."

He tried to push out a laugh, but only smiled. "Well, I do. What if the answer is that there's nothing to do with my life? My whole life is just going through motions without committing to anything?"

"Robert, that's simply not true. I look through your eyes every time I see you. Behind them, I can see the inner workings of the universe. You know it, too. You wouldn't be such an outsider all the time if you were meant to get lost in the crowd."

She sensed how weary he was and rolled off of him. They both lay on the roof looking up at the sky that looked exactly as it did when they came out, yet it kept churning and changing as they watched. They lost track of time, but each knew separately that they weren't going anywhere that night. Marie broke the silence. "Are you always this hard on yourself? Always carrying the worries of the entire world on your shoulders?"

With his eyes locked on the glowing, orange sky, he answered: "Yes."

She asked the question so that he could hear his own answer to it. Once she was certain that Robert knew the weight of his response, she got up. As she passed over him, she broke whatever spell the sky had cast on him and he trailed her through the window to her bedroom. With no more words, Robert undressed and went to bed. Throughout the house, Marie locked up and turned lights out.

Robert closed his eyes and saw the stress and tension of his mind begin to break under its own pressure and crack with electric-blue flashes. He tried to stay awake to watch the phosphenes, as if they were lightning from a distant storm, but he began drifting in the comfort of knowing that his anxieties and worries were blinking out of existence. With each flash, they blurred his reality. The further he drifted into sleep, the faster and brighter they flashed, until finally, with one sudden rush, he let go of consciousness and fell through the phosphenes into sleep.

6

When Robert woke, Marie was gone. The smell of coffee was the only thing his mind could anchor to while his thoughts ebbed and flowed with the chaos of an unsettled shore. A slow headache began pulsating, as if signaling from a distant star. He sensed it was late in the day, but wasn't sure how long he had slept until he tried moving and the stiffness his body made it difficult to swing his legs over the side of the bed. Through the window he saw a familiar twilit sky, and then he scanned the room as he gained his senses. It had a less welcoming air to it than it did last night, and he couldn't decide whether Marie had cleaned while he was sleeping or if she actually *was* packing. A slight charge of panic stirred at the thought of her leaving, but it flashed out of him as he thought of the blue flashes that released so many of his worries last night.

On the edge of the bed, he closed his eyes with his head in his hands and tried to mentally fall through the phosphenes once more to reach through to the memory of a dream, but it was impossible. He slept so hard that he must have purged any memory of dreams from existence. His mind was too exhausted from stress to start the day with anxiety and worrying about Marie leaving. He pushed the idea out of his thoughts, trying to blue-flash it out of existence. Knowing too well that he wouldn't be able to keep the small doubts in his mind from taking hold, he got up and went to find her so that her presence would occupy his thoughts and keep any anxieties at bay.

Downstairs, he found no signs of Marie other than a pot of coffee. He helped himself and went outside to smoke and found that Marie was already sitting on the steps, reading a book with a cigarette and coffee. She turned at the sound of the door opening. "Hey."

Robert sat next to her. She held out the last of her cigarette instead of flicking it into the street so that he could start his from it. He started his cigarette and flicked hers away. "I'm sorry I slept so long, but thanks for letting me do it."

She leaned into his shoulder. "You obviously needed it. How are you?"

He had a headache from too much sleep and the coffee and cigarette were working a knot into his empty stomach. "I feel like I slept for fifteen hours." He half-joked and then answered her real question. "I'm tired of thinking about everything, but I guess it's unavoidable."

Marie was slow to reply. "It is." She squeezed his arm for a moment before going back into the house. She returned with a takeout box and a pot of coffee in her hands and a book bag slung over her shoulder. She placed the food and coffee on the steps and then locked the front door. Robert dug into the food while Marie stood on the sidewalk at the bottom of the steps, drinking her coffee and proclaiming her plans for the evening. She had been his caretaker for the past twenty-four hours. She had let him explore his thoughts with her, let him sleep as long as he needed, and then fed and caffeinated him. As she playfully laid it out for him, whether or not he liked it, he was at her disposal, and they were going to proceed with the previous night's plans and make their way out to the campsite. With the euphoria of a headache driven out by food and caffeine, he was in no position to object. Marie traded one of last night's bottles of vodka for his empty coffee mug. She placed the mugs by the door and walked down the steps into the middle of the street. "Let's go. Forget about everything and give into the night."

With acceptance, Robert got up from the steps and joined her by her side as they walked down the middle of the dead street, ready to conquer the night. The sun had fully set as they made their way, like silent warriors, down the orange-lit corridors until they boarded a train. Seated next to each other and armed against the other passengers with their bottles of vodka, they rode as if they were existing in a distinct reality from the rest of the world. The vodka was their secret that separated them from the others. They drank it and shared subtle smiles with each other as the other passengers remained clueless to their game and rode the train through the doldrums of life. Marie reached down into her bag and withdrew a book of Beat poetry. She handed the open bag to Robert for him to choose. Watching him finger through the titles as if their fates depended upon it, she smiled as he plucked out a well-worn copy of an absurdist play. She released a sigh of relief that Robert wouldn't be distilling his thoughts and becoming pensive on the train ride and would hopefully give up some of his prudence to how absurd the world is. Maybe he would even be in a laughing mood by the time they reached their destination.

As the two read and drank, the factories were relentless. Unlike on the ride to the sea, the factories never broke away from view to give the passengers any insight into the local life. There were no side streets lined with bars or shops to peer down. It seemed like they were traveling down an endless gauntlet of industry with the only relief being offered as the tracks rose above the factories and revealed the expanse of industry as it ran out towards the horizon. The change of pattern out the window got Robert's attention. He took a moment to look up from the book, and as the story dissolved, his own thoughts began creeping in. He imagined all the processes that must be taking place in the factories as they stretched out. His mind saw sheets of metal being folded and shaped. He imagined various parts of their train swirling along factory conveyors in an endless assembly line, with all the processes moving in sync to some mysterious muted music. He could hear the rumbling motors and smell the charged industrial dust. For a moment he was comforted by the order.

As quickly as it began, his affinity towards industry wore off and his displeasure towards all of it took over. He stopped picturing the mesmerizing nexus inside the factories and focused on the rooftops and smokestacks framed by the window. He thought of the smoke and steam as more than just pollution—he imagined the dreams of the workers being destroyed and then vented out. He wondered if the pollution he saw really was that spiritual and if the dream-routed workers could one day be reunited with their passions. There was a tinge of depression, thinking about whether or not the dreams waited on people, as if after all their struggles, they could one day attain enlightenment and be swept away in a grand realization of everything they had lost. Or maybe the dreams were vented out of Earth's atmosphere into the cold expanse of space, and the workers died as far from their dreams as the planet had traveled since they lost them. Robert glanced at Marie, took a shot of vodka, and returned to his book with no more thought of it. He hoped he could fall back into the story fast enough that the depressing thoughts would vaporize in his short-term memory before they could contribute to his mood.

Off the train, it was the same scene as it had been all along the way. There were minor differences in the architecture of the train station and of the buildings out across the street, but to anyone who wasn't familiar, this station could have been confused with any other station of industry. They exited the station with the other passengers before Marie jolted Robert out of his intention to follow the design and pulled him around the side of the building. Once there, they ducked through a chain-link fence and Robert noticed the strange sensation of walking over dirt instead of the concrete and asphalt that his feet were accustomed to. Although absent under the soles of his boots, the concrete was present in abundance in a canopy that jutted out from the station, with what seemed like a grand purpose for a few hundred yards before abruptly breaking off in the sky.

Robert was sure of an increase in pressure as they followed a path through the trees into what became a valley that sunk like a chasm under the sea. Marie explained, "They cleared the way for a train line to go through, but never finished building the tracks. The project was halted, but because the railway still owns the land, the factories weren't able to creep in. There are still no stars, but it at least provides the illusion of being out in nature."

Robert said nothing, but adjusted to his surroundings as they persisted through the valley. The sterile and synthetic smells of industry dissipated and gave way to the ozone refreshment of pine and dirt, which was soon fumigated with wood-smoke and the punk smell of human activity. The pair traveled through the darkness until the valley walls were cast in an orange hue from small campfires on the way down. As Robert and Marie went deeper, the settlement became more dense with activity. The music, which further up seemed jumbled, started to sync up as people got closer together and tuned to the same station. The soundtrack to the activity began to intoxicate Robert. The trees were a blazing orange on either side of the valley, and the dancing women cast shadows on them. The rhythmic thirty-foot sirens seduced Robert. He watched them in a trance as he descended deeper, before finally returning his gaze to Marie. She was guiding him by his hand, not so much as to lead him but to protect him from the others. Robert was an outsider here. He knew these people, drank at their bars, and went to their shows—but that was different. That was on industrialized land. They may have occupied the buildings, but industrial zones would always be Robert's territory. The others merely took up space on industrial grounds, while Robert's energy resonated with every Brutalist atom.

With his feet in the dirt, Robert was detached from industry and with no conduit to channel its energy to him. He thought of Marie as an amulet guiding him through the judgement of the others. The sirens of seduction were obscured and forgotten from his peripheral as he fell under Marie's enchantment. The larger fires ahead of them lit her outline with a bright orange glow that highlighted her curves and set her hair ablaze. He was consumed by her ethereal figure. The heat and energy from the fires and activity around them seemed to be only radiating from her. He forgot everything and everyone. His vision went black except for the fire that was Marie as she protected him and guided him further down and deeper under the pressure of the sea, but he recognized too intimately that the pressure was the projected thoughts of the others.

    The angle of decline leveled out, and as it forced Robert and Maire to change their pace, it also forced Robert out of his enchantment. With reluctance, he allowed Marie's glow to dissipate and materialize to become the world around them. The dead-end of the valley they found themselves in was the main circle of activity. The music had changed from the radio stations up the hill and was coming out of speakers all around. Although he couldn't find the source, he recognized that the music was not commercial, and that someone was at the source and in control of the mood it determined. Conscious of this, Robert constructed mental barriers, and, with a scorching scrutiny, surveyed the surrounding scene. The judging faces on him were as intense as the heat from the massive bonfire. A thread of anger spiraled its way from Robert's chest to his throat. The longer he focused on how they observed him, the tighter it constricted until it began squeezing adrenaline into his veins. The adrenaline mixed with the vodka already in his system and acted as a strange drug. The music and weed fumes in the air slowly fogged his mind. He again detached from reality, but instead of following his contempt toward the others, he pivoted his emotions towards Marie's wish that he give into the night. He didn't plan on interacting with the others much to begin with. He had firmly resolved that he was there to spend time with Maire and that he was going to have a good time with her. He took this moment of escape to reset himself. He didn't want a repeat of last night; he was too exhausted with the tension and turmoil of his mind to put any more energy into it. He gave into the warmth of the atmosphere and let his objections melt away.

A large log was thrown on the fire, and with a great flash, the embers sent sparks up into the night. Robert's eyes followed them on their ascent. The trees were so bright from the fire that it made the sky look black, as if the usual, orange-lit sky had cracked open to reveal the black void beyond. The sparks swirled higher and resembled the stars and galaxies in the distance. The final galaxies burnt, the universes ended, and their dead ashes slowly sank back to Earth. A single ash caught Robert's eye as it softly fell and rested on Marie's shoulder. He brushed it off and caressed her to establish a physical connection with the surrounding reality. She turned to him and made eye contact just before they were interrupted by someone offering them drinks. Robert accepted a bottle of beer and braced himself for the interactions that were to come as random people approached and talked with Marie. He drank and was friendly enough the few times it was necessary, but he ached to have Marie alone. He didn't want to leave the party, but he wanted it to be just the two of them together with the party going on around them.

With Marie engaged in conversation, Robert's attention drifted and began scanning the faces around the fire. The only familiar face that he finally came upon was Lucy's. He was relieved when the sight of her didn't stir up any charged emotions. As he watched her, he contemplated their past and wondered why it had caused so much turmoil within him, but without coming to any real conclusions, he let the task go. He figured it was best to forget. Whether to blame her or his own mental health for using her as a catalyst for depression and anger didn't matter to him; the pain and anxiety attached to her was gone, and that was all that mattered. He noticed that none of the positive emotions towards her remained either; that must have been the price of purging the negative ones. He couldn't stir up any of the things that had attracted him to her in the first place, but he also couldn't bring himself to hate her. He had gotten what he wanted and was neutral; she was just another familiar face.

As he came out of reflection, Lucy made eye contact with him from across the fire, and with a natural movement, he raised a hand to her. She exchanged the gesture with a smile that turned into action once she saw Marie. Robert braced himself as Lucy approached. He was in no fear of anything she might stir up in him, as he was confident he was in control of those emotions, but he was possessive of the emotions he had been experiencing with Marie. He didn't want to share them with the outside world. It was easy for him to write off everyone else at the party; he didn't know them too well, and he didn't care about them, but Lucy was familiar, and he was afraid she might penetrate the walls he put up and gain access to what he hoped would remain private.

Lucy invited him and Marie to sit with her group around one of the smaller campfires. She either didn't notice they had arrived together or didn't care. Her neutral concern came so naturally. It confirmed everything Robert had come to conclude. Without the alarms of anxiety sounding off in his mind at the presence of Lucy, and with relief that he could keep Marie to himself, Robert eased the edge off his defenses and followed Lucy.

Sitting at the campfire that Lucy had led him to, Robert learned everything he needed to know about the small mob running through the streets at the piers and setting the train cars on fire. The entire party was really more of a headquarters for their mock revolution. It was set up like a military outpost, with the key players down at the bonfire and the soldiers camping out all the way up the hill. He learned of their plans and unexpectedly learned of Marie's involvement in the protests. The plan was to block the delivery of the new automated machines. Robert was going to correct them that the machines were already in place, but it was more satisfying to know something that they did not. He nervously waited for Marie to step in and correct them, but she never did. Robert received a great wave of gratitude knowing that the conversations he had with her were between only the two of them. The protective spirit that led him down through the valley had protected him once more. He was beyond humble. With the new energy and fondness for Marie surging within him, he wished he could find a way to express it in that very moment, but the most he could do was place a hand between her shoulders and hope that some of the energy would pulse through her. She seemed to understand and returned his gesture by putting her hand above his knee and squeezing just enough to pulse some energy back.

His attention returned to the misinformed faux revolutionaries. They frustrated him; it was like hearing Jack's nonsense but from a different angle. He put these people's opinions in the same category as the opinions he heard at The Bounty. Robert couldn't believe that they didn't see it on the train ride in; just to get to this campsite showed the massive scale of industry. He scoffed at how ridiculous it was that these people expected to change something that stretched so far out from their eyes that it took on its own entity.

The more the conversation went on, the more Lucy and the others wanted Robert's take on it all. He was the only one who had actually been *inside* the factories, but he didn't want to talk about it. The questions were asked with a condescending attitude, as if every moment spent in that factory wasn't a moment that he was contemplating his own existence. He only hoped that after Marie had learned of his thoughts, she would see how absurd these people were. Lucy pressed on, but he didn't want to argue with anyone about the politics of the workforce's place in society or how his paycheck-to-paycheck lifestyle didn't fit their worldview. He dodged the main questions until, finally, the group realized they would not get much out of him. He did his best not to let the experience alter his mood, and once they left him alone, the conversation went on with a biased fury among the more excited members. Robert tuned them out and stayed comfortably close to Marie. He drank and watched the fire dance through his cigarette smoke. The people around him, although they weren't his favorite type, were providing enough energy for Robert to pretend he was in the mix and having an enjoyable time. People came and went, and then mostly went, and Robert was finally alone with Marie.

Robert did not want to have a serious conversation, but he had to ask a serious question before he could let it go. "Did you know they were going to be at the piers the other night? Is that why we went?"

Marie was blindsided by the question and sat straight up. "No. No, I knew they had been planning something at the trains, but I had no idea we'd be running into them. How could I? Seeing you was spontaneous, I thought about the stars and wanted to show them to you."

Robert couldn't take it anymore. Everything

always weighed so heavily on his mind. He was upset with himself for even asking, yet relieved to hear the answer. He couldn't spare any more energy towards serious thoughts. He tried to find a way out, thought of mocking the protestors, but instead went with the truth.

"I didn't mean to bring down the mood. You know a thought like that would grow and torture me if I didn't ask it."

As if she could sense that Robert needed a way out from his heavy thoughts, she got up, sat on his lap, and kissed him. She then dug a pack of cigarettes out of his pocket, started two, and put one on Robert's lip. The neurons in Robert's mind went erratic. He thought of how Lucy's interest was always to have him as a novelty, but never to commit to anything serious. She would never show him the attention in public that she would show him in private. For Marie to show this kind of affection in front of all the people that Lucy hid him from showed him she was real—any lingering fears he had about her vaporized.

She looked him in the eyes and saw that she had accomplished her mission. She got up, found two bottles of beer, gave one to Robert, and then sat back at his side.

In a rejuvenated mood of happiness, he playfully asked, "So, this is one of your projects? The great revolution?"

She was happily shocked by his mocking tone. "*One* of them, yes. I don't get as electrified about the politics of it all as they do, but I have a surplus of art supplies, and they needed signs for their cause. You know, people do actually have fun taking part in things."

Robert nodded. "They don't even realize that's why they do it. None of this is going to have any effect on automation, but they'll remember the fun they had playing protestors."

Marie leaned back in her chair and gave him a playful shove. "Let them be. If they're as ineffective as you think they are, then they won't be hurting anybody. They might even learn from it and come around to your wisdom."

He laughed at the idea of being wise.

The night continued to pass as the conversion remained playful between them. Eventually, after they drank their fill, they wandered off through the trees and found a soft patch of grass in a clearing where they could escape the noise of the party behind them. To their surprise, the end of the valley broke off over cliffs and they were actually high above the factories. From their vantage point, they could see the rolling hills of industry sprawling out in every direction. The bright orange lights looked like neurons communicating across an enormous network. Robert wondered if everything he saw was shut down and being automated; his mind couldn't conceive an army of machines on that scale. He looked to the right and could just barely make out a dark line that must have been the ocean before it plunged over the horizon. He tried to imagine the piers from the other night stretched along the coast of the continent. It seemed impossible that the same scenario was occurring throughout the expanse before him. He was too drunk to try and find any sense in it. He looked straight ahead at the factories with their steady streams of smoke and steam billowing up towards the churning orange sky. The entire scene, from the streets up to the sky, looked like a single entity primed and waiting to come to life. He was in no state to philosophize what his eyes saw, so he laid down next to Maire in the grass.

* * * * *

In the late morning, Robert and Marie laid together on their backs and watched the sky as their eyes picked up on the tiny dots that shot in and out of existence. These sky sprites danced through the firmament as if putting on a performance for them. Robert wished they would gently fall down on him like spiritual snow. He hadn't wished out of depression or a desire to see their destruction, but he hoped that through their pressure he could discover their reality. He wanted a physical connection with his ideas about the universe. Marie was content to watch them shoot in and out of existence and thought of the world with people coming and going. The weightless dance of the sprites let them both let go of any heavy thoughts in their minds.

Robert spoke first. "Overcast. When the sky wasn't orange above the trees, I had hoped we had gone out far enough to get out from under the constant cover. Is everywhere overcast?"

"Not where I'm going." She squeezed his hand, and it pulsed a slight sense of alarm up his arm and into his neck, but neither of them moved. They continued to watch the sprites.

"Going? where?" He realized she hadn't loosened her grip; he knew it meant there was something coming, and he braced himself.

"I've been given an opportunity, and I'm afraid I have to take it. If I stay here, I'll never progress. I've outgrown my schooling here."

Robert wished the sky sprites really would gain mass and drop on him. He wanted the sky to fall; he wanted stones on his chest. He wanted physical pain to match his reeling emotions. Exhausted from emotion, he wanted only physical pain.

He managed to get out "Okay..." before his voice wavered.

He would not lead himself into a depression. He knew their time together was limited. He never looked too far into the future, and in that respect, he gave no thought to a future with her. He gave up any attempt to find an emotion and tried to detach and exist within the firmament above. He looked through it until he was engulfed by it.

He gave up the notion of asking her how long they'd be apart, how far away she would be, or if they would ever be together again as a couple. Somehow, he knew the answers to these questions didn't matter. He didn't quite know why, but he knew. He propped himself on one arm and ran fingers through her hair as he took in the sight of her. He knew no remorse.

After a long look through Robert's eyes, Marie spoke. "We'll always be connected somehow. We could be on either side of the planet and the connection would cut straight through the Earth's core. When I think of you, I'll be filtering reality through your eyes and thoughts, and that's all it will take to be together. We could never meet again, yet we would still exist for each other."

Although their time together had been short, it was intense enough to mark them both forever. The entire time she spoke, he had been taking in her features and absorbing her beauty. He experienced no insult, no depression, no anger. He couldn't conjure up rejection or jealousy. There was absolutely nothing negative towards Marie that he could sense in any fiber of his being. He looked into her eyes, and without knowing their depth, he knew they had the ability to engulf him. He then closed his eyes, and with a sense of falling, he lowered his forehead to meet hers.

Their worlds went silent. She closed her eyes and the physical world around them dissolved. In their blinded darkness, they shed their physical bodies. They detached from the earth and floated in their tiny place in the dark expanse of the universe as they slowly drifted together through the Ether. They existed for each other in a perfect moment.

This moment they could always return to for the rest of their lives; they could always be together, always know each other, always see the world through their unique filter as if the other were standing right next to them. Future conditions of a million different paths from this moment would have no influence over their connection. Nothing existed on the same level. Their spiritual beings plunged into the collective unconsciousness of humanity and would be able to forever meet on a plain that few knew existed.

Robert opened his eyes and pulled back his head as if waking from a dream. He looked into Marie's opening eyes, and for a moment, before fully returning to their bodily senses, she looked different, as if her human form couldn't quite contain her stellar beauty. He lingered in the spiritual world for one last deep breath and exhale before lowering himself down to kiss her. Her lips were hot, and they knew nothing else had to be said. No sadness would exist in their parting; they would only know joy from each other. Robert laid back by her side and breathed in the scent of her hair; it conjured the memory of when she had hidden in his hoodie during the police chase. He breathed in again and imagined every detail down to the tear gas. With her by his side, he closed his eyes and practiced living in a memory of her.

Soon, however, the smell of tear gas became too real to ignore. Robert and Marie were jolted out of their peace by unfamiliar sounds filtering through the trees. They went towards the noise and broke through the tree line to the commotion of the cops clearing everyone out. Without too much resistance, the protestors and party-goes began trekking up the hill and leaving the scene. A few stragglers tried to stand their ground—some were met with shouting, while others were met with violence.

The officer that seemed in charge removed his gas mask and began shouting, "This is railroad property. Vacate immediately!"

With the shouting and violence growing, Robert wasted no time taking Marie's hand and leading her up the valley. In a reversal of last night, he became her protector; his clothes were work clothes and looked less threatening to the cops than the look of the protestors. The cops hardly paid them any attention as they granted the pair free travel while harassing the bohemians and hipsters. Without looking back, Robert and Marie could hear the tensions rising behind them. The energy surged and rushed them up the hill, where they ducked under the fence and entered the station.

They boarded the first train heading back home. It was full of excitement and repeated opinions from around the bonfire, only louder and with more conviction than the night before. To escape some of the excitement, Robert found a seat in the back of the car and let Marie in first so that he could act as a buffer between her and the others. Marie tried to lose herself looking out the window. In complete contrast to the energy on the train, the gray factories and steam looked docile. She imagined the electricity from the tracks was charging the passengers and getting them worked up. It seemed like everyone had to take their turn and make a speech about the cops and the automation of the factories. Robert clenched his teeth, trying not to let their words penetrate. They were angry and excited after a confrontation; he let it go at that and tuned them out. He looked out the window with Marie, resistant to the energy that rode with them.

The further the train carried them from the cops, the more the energy drained from the crowd. The mini protest had lost most of its momentum, with only a few concerned riders still philosophizing among themselves. By the time they got back home, the ride was like any other, except filled with an abundance of weary travelers for the hour. After waiting for the car to clear, Robert and Marie exited in exhaustion and made their way to Robert's apartment —his was the closest, and with only a few hours of sleep, they went the nearest bed to sleep off some of the experience before confronting it.

Before they fell asleep, Marie went to her bag and brought the book of Beat poetry she was reading back with her to bed. She straddled Robert and pushed it to his chest. "I'll carry you in my mind like a book that I can open up and fall into whenever I want to. Keep this and fall into it when you want to be with me."

She then rolled off to lie by his side with one

hand still holding the book. Robert put his hand over hers and looked over at her while she slept. He wanted to draw her near, as if to catch the emotion falling from her to soften her departure. Instead, he closed his eyes. As he fell asleep, he knew it would be the last time he would see her.

7

Robert woke with the entire world weighing down on him. Marie was gone again, only this time there was no lingering sense of her teasing him with her presence. In her place was the book she left, and in looking at it, he knew her absence was final. He knew it would be no use trying to chase her down; she had probably finished packing and left town already. He thought of what it would be like if she were next to him now and how they might have interpreted the scene at the campsite together. He thought of her this way until he reached a point where it would do more damage than good. In an attempt to flee his emotions, he left the room and left his thoughts of her behind.

The sky beyond the sliding glass door was orange and twilit. *At least one thing in my life is constant*, he thought as he slid the door open and stepped outside to smoke. While thinking of work, he looked out at the blinking lights on the orange smokestacks and exhaled his own smoke in their direction. He wasn't sure what kind of job he would return to or whether there would be any job at all waiting for him. He figured the best thing to do would be to head down to The Bounty and get an update on the factories.

Without urgency to leave, he went back inside for a beer and then continued to smoke on the balcony. He could smell the campfire on his clothes and hair and worked a shower into his routine of smoking and drinking. The shower recharged him, and his clothes became his armor; he wore his work boots and pants and swapped his smoke-filled hoodie for his work jacket. By the third beer and cigarette, he began to get anxious about leaving. If he stayed where he was, he would think too much about Marie. He was already reliving moments with her and decided it was time to get going before negative thoughts began clouding his mind. He knew that eventually he could accomplish what they agreed upon and visit her in his mind with comfort, but until that day came, any thought of her was going to be difficult. It was going to require work on his part to exhaust any pain associated with her absence before he could be rewarded. Whether or not he would one day derive joy from her didn't matter now; she had left him, and the first symptoms of rejection were taking hold in him. In order to escape his tendency towards disappointment, he should leave. He went back inside to get her book and put it in his back pocket. He hoped that at some point in the night he might fall into it and be comforted or, more likely, begin the work of dealing with the pain. He knew if this moment happened without the book that his missed opportunity might become his downfall and set off a chain reaction of a deeper depression.

On his way to The Bounty, the Brutalist buildings seemed to jut out over the street at odd angles as Robert walked. At times, he thought they might lose their footing and topple over him. He looked up and tried to discern whether they were occupied. For all their sterile and industrial appeal, he found it hard to believe that any life could flourish in them. If anyone was inside them, they must be as severe as the buildings they occupied. Their lonely abandonment seemed incapable of supporting anyone with a joyful life.

Throughout the corridor, the warm-winded energy of an approaching storm picked up momentum. The buildings were unwavering and stood their ground as long gusts pushed the leaves and litter down the streets. Robert pushed against them with short bursts of leaning forward. He turned his back towards the wind and watched the debris tumble down the street. As he turned around to face forward again, The Bounty just came into sight.

Instead of a rise in anticipation, he knew something was wrong. The Bounty seemed lifeless; the usual sounds penetrating the walls were silent, and no light gleamed from within. The energy that usually resonated through the sidewalk and street and ran its way up the feet and legs of the passerby was completely still. An emptiness formed in Robert's chest. He pulled on the front door that wouldn't budge, and his breath collapsed.

In disbelief, he tried the door a few more times. Still not believing, he made his way around the side and back of the bar. It was unheard of; as long as he had been around, he never knew of The Bounty being closed. It was a landmark. It was a beacon that stood for the factory workers when everything else in their lives let them down. That The Bounty was closed seemed impossible. Robert couldn't imagine where everyone was. His sense of rejection intensified. It was inconceivable that they all left town without telling him; of all the patrons, he was the least likely to stick around. He could find factory work anywhere, so he didn't care if his factory failed; it was the other workers that had no choices; it was the old men that needed pensions; it was the miserably ordinary people with no futures that were going to live in the factories forever—not *him*.

The more he thought about rejection, the more he transformed it into rage. In a flash, he hated everyone that could think to reject him or abandon him to the situation and leave him in their wake. He tried to regain logic by rushing from his reeling emotions back to the front of the bar. He anxiously looked up and down the street for some place to find shelter. With his feet already in motion, his eyes targeted a phone booth, and he decided he would call Jack. He closed the door to protect himself against the wind and emotions, dropped the coins in, and dialed Jack's number. Inside the isolated chamber, the empty ringing of Jack's line echoed against the glass. Even with him inside, the phone booth seemed to contain an emptiness beyond hollow. He listened to each ring as it came off the glass and resonated within the negative space. With each ring, Robert became more troubled. After more than enough time, he put the phone back on its cradle and rested his head on the back of his hand.

He couldn't figure out where everyone was. He felt like he was in a dream of empty streets with the invisible demons of his mental health chasing him down. The longer he couldn't figure out the present moment, the more the pressure of not being able to figure out his life crushed him. He couldn't stand it in the phone booth any longer. He knew he needed to find direction before he was engulfed with emotion. He decided on his next move; he couldn't go back home and drink alone—it would only welcome depression. The Bounty was out; he certainly would not break in and drink alone. The only option he had at his disposal was to go to the District where the bars were and to drink with the type of people that were at the campsite last night. He couldn't stand to be alone tonight and thought he might be able to get lost in the crowd. He knew that if he could numb himself for a little while, he might take some control back.

He lingered in the phone booth a little longer to steady himself, but the storm kept approaching. The wind put a strain on the structure and slowly rocked it back and forth. Robert's mind fell into the rhythm and conjured up dream-like visions. He could sense his emotions looming over him and imagined them as a kettle of giant vultures slowing spiraling overhead. The trash and debris in the street mimicked their spiral on the concrete that surrounded him. He watched the litter dance around him as he thought of the predatory emotions waiting for him outside. He saw each article as representing a different thought. To a crumpled newspaper, he attached the possibility of going to the District. In a paper cup he saw Marie leaving, and in a candy-wrapper fluttering down the street he saw the empty Bounty. As he visualized his thoughts, he tried to grab hold of one and make a decision. He watched the newspaper break from the spiral and flutter towards the direction of the District. He broke free from his own spiraling thoughts and tried to play out what would happen if he went there. He wouldn't be alone, and hopefully being around that many people would be enough of a distraction that his emotions couldn't take hold. He stood alone in the quiet phone booth, looking up at the circling emotions that were waiting for him to exit. The orange clouds churned above him, and as the factory lights on the smokestacks flashed like lightning, he swore he could actually see dark, winged emotions spiraling over him, waiting for a moment of weakness to strike. A surge of worry ran through him and filled the booth. He had always regarded his stronger emotions as inner devastations. His fear of what was to come if those emotions got him began to work in his mind, harder than any amount of alcohol ever could. As his worry and fear filled the booth to capacity and began fogging the glass, he decided to make a break for it. For a moment, he was seized by panic before bursting out.

Drugged with emotion, Robert began bolting down the street towards the safety of the District. He sensed the predatory emotions take chase and pursue him down the corridor. As the wind kicked up and pushed him back, they struck. First, a charge of anxiety swooped down on him to electrify and sensitize his nerves before returning to the kettle. The charged ions from the coming storm ran through his body and levitated dust off the ground. Next, a bolt of depression struck him, knocking him forward. As he stumbled to gain his footing, his body got heavier. His movements slowed as he pushed and strained his muscles to move faster. He pushed with all his energy, but it wasn't enough. All at once, jealousy, shame, and disgust dove down on him. His mind clanged like a gong and dropped him to his knees. Disgusted with himself, he hesitated to get up. With one knee on the concrete, he looked forward. He could see the lights of the District ahead, he could smell the bars and see the people, but it was too late. He wouldn't be able to find the shelter he sought in the crowd. Enough negative emotion had taken hold of him that it dictated his actions. He braced himself as he invited the next emotions to take hold. The shadow overtook him before it struck. The razor-sharp talons took hold of his shoulder blades and charged him— one side with anger and the other with self-loathing. They devastated him; he could no longer control his emotions nor contain them. The only thing he could do was project them. He entered the District and all he could do was hate. All his convictions of himself, he began pushing towards other people. He entered one of the buildings and sat at the bar to brood. Everything in him was wrong, so he began picking apart other people. He judged their every action. He realized that everything he had inside himself was something he could see in them, and so he began to self-destruct. He thought he could destroy them by destroying himself. The more he hurt himself, the more it would expose the others. He drank with a self-destructive purpose to feed the demons and smite everyone around him.

    Robert continued this way at the bar for a few rounds, but for all it did, it didn't seem to fulfill his intentions. He decided one bar wouldn't do and that he would go from bar to bar until he hated everyone in the District. With a distinct atmosphere in every bar, he found new things to destroy about the different people he saw. If he went to a bar that was joyful, then he drank to destroy his happiness within. If he went to a bar that was artful, he drank to destroy the hopes that his creativity would save him from a boring life. He found a dive bar that was tough and edgy, and so he drank hard to mock himself and destroy the notion that any act he put on made him tougher. At the intellectual bar, he wanted to drink himself into a stupor, but the reeling charged emotions wouldn't allow it. They had taken hold, and alcohol was no match for them. He had all the physical symptoms of being drunk, but something deep inside his mind was keeping it sober. The negative emotions weren't even slightly numbed and were driving him to further self-destruction as strongly as when they had begun.

With defeat, he left the District and wandered the streets. A migraine, as if summoned by his emotions, came to life and worked to push the drunk out of his mind. It was incredible; the emotions that controlled so much of his life by proxy had now actually taken a physical hold in his brain and pushed all the slow, sludgy drunkenness out of his mind. In disbelief, he was slowly becoming incapacitated by the pain and sudden sobriety. He could only squint and touch the buildings as a guide until the familiar sight of a food truck came into view. He approached and bought a black coffee. He sat on a concrete picnic table with his feet on the bench as he closed his eyes and drank. When he was done with it, he ordered another. The first cup of coffee worked at his migraine, and the second made him able to smoke a cigarette. His senses sharpened and the pulsating pain shrank down to a tiny pinprick. By the end of the second cup, he could open his eyes and move around again. There was a soreness as he moved his eyes, but it was nowhere near the crippling pain of a migraine. He got a third cup and began walking.

He thought the migraine had only eclipsed the numbing effects of alcohol, but as the caffeine pushed it out of the way, he realized it had vaporized all the work the drunk had done. He was left again with nothing but anger at himself and the world around him. The cigarette smoke began fogging his mind once again with self-destruction as he walked with no direction.

The tension held in the wind finally broke, and the rain came down on Robert. He wondered if it was true rain or if the condensate from the factories had thickened enough to fall back down on him. Either way mattered little to him, as both forms would contain the polluted exhaust from the factories. A greasy film of the moisture formed on his skin; it was surely too tainted to be natural and felt artificial and grimy. As he walked through what he imagined as a dystopian and industrialized rainforest, depression thickened within him—the depression of being cut off from future possibilities. He had knowledge that not everything was possible for him; not all opportunities would be extended towards him. He would never travel the world, he would never explore a real rainforest, he would know nothing of the good fortune of experiencing the unexpected possibilities that a favorable universe would put in order for him. The knowledge of some of his futures being extinguished made it possible for more to burn out. He flipped his collar up against the rain and stuffed his fists deep into his pockets as his chest got tight and the walls of his future closed in on him.

He imagined the sky as a free plain where the vapor in the clouds represented all possible future versions of himself. As his dreams became improbable, they condensed and fell to earth. He began considering his dreams as being as harmful as the pollution the factories spewed out. The more it rained, the more his future became finite and singular. He walked as his dreams rained down around him, leaving nothing but despair in the skies and toxic streams of reality that would slowly erode, pollute, and poison his world. His dreams fell through the exhausted dreams of the other factory workers and combined to create an acid rain of despair. Some of it mixed with the coffee he drank. The taste made him scoff at the idea of his dreams once again rejoining him. This communion of hope made everything worse and magnified his depression. He wished he could use his depression as an absolute cleansing, but the idea of hope spoiled it. Residues from his dreams and ambitions always clung to him in the form of hope after he thought he had purged them from his mind. Even if the rain were natural and cleansed some toxicity from the skies as it passed through and took some hope with it, the people were never truly free from it. The skies may seem brighter, but the drinking water was poisoned. Instead of relief as his depression cleared his mind of improbable dreams and distilled them into rational realities, the poison of hope was in him and would dictate his future actions to hold him back from achieving things possible in reality. He thought about how hope acted like a curse. His depression could be dealt with swiftly if not for hope preventing it from detaching from his mind. He hated hope; he resented it. As he drank his black, acid-rain coffee, he consumed all hope and incinerated it in what was becoming a raging furnace in his heart. Robert focused on his rage; he fed it with all his energy. He imagined it burning so hot that the rain would instantly boil and steam away before touching his body. His anger burned stronger than his depression and soon took over. He created armor around him that nothing could penetrate. He didn't know where he was heading, but he was going to set the night on fire and drink himself into oblivion.

The first shop he entered was familiar and in it he realized exactly what he was going to do. Marie took him to this store before they went to the piers. He could think of nothing as cold and lonely as trying to recreate a happy moment in a state of despair and depression. He wanted to face his painful emotions, and with no hesitation, he found two bottles of the same wine that they drank that night. In the same style as Marie, he uncorked the bottles and bought her brand of cigarettes. As he walked out, he threw the plastic wineglasses in the trash. He was going to relive their best night together to destroy it. Only at the other end of pain would he find joy.

On his walk to the train station, he began drinking off the first wine bottle. The reintroduction of alcohol into his system rejuvenated his drunk. It focused and intensified his anger. He saw that the spot the food truck had previously occupied was vacant, and his sense of rejection burned brighter in his furnace as he passed it with fury. He walked over the grate that he and Marie had synchronically flicked their cigarettes into and started a cigarette upon entering the station. He blew smoke at the turnstile, where he swiped his metro card and then threw it off to the side instead of pocketing it. If he had no way back, he didn't care. He wanted to face difficulties head on. He invited them as he chased a ghost of Marie down the train vault to the platform. He flicked his cigarette at the oncoming train and wished he could destroy his emotions the same way the red sparks exploded.

Riding the train, Robert drank and looked out at the factories. He imagined their automated processes continuing without him. Rejection blazed within. The factories had abandoned him the same way everyone else did. They would continue without him as if he had never mattered. The sky churned orange, and he hated it. He wished it would rip open and drop flaming hail on the factories. The heat of the burning factories penetrated through the glass before the train entered the station at the end of the line.

Drunk on city lights and high on factory fumes, Robert exited the station. The rain persisted as he pressed on through the deluge of dead dreams. He thought of actual dreams that he had had while he slept; whether they were good or bad, they always wrapped him in love. As he woke and a dream died, the pain of the world crept in, and he always wished he could fall back asleep and be engulfed by love again. Following the path that he and Marie had walked; he had died a thousand dreams. He knew complete annihilation, looking down the street and watching the torrents of his dreams obliterated upon the pavement. Marie wanted to show him the stars. He was ready to see them and command them to rain down on him, too. He imagined the stars above the orange canopy and wished they would drop and crush reality. With no response to his wishes, the sky continued to churn as it always had. Rejected by the sky, Robert traversed the boardwalk until he arrived at the seawall.

He walked out into the sea with the water and energy rising around him. Drunk and swaying down the path as waves pounded against both sides of the wall, he mimicked the sea and swayed to the rhythm of the surrounding waves. The orange industrial sky diffused and darkened as he went out with nothing but the orange streetlight at the end of the pier. It was calling like a siren. He focused on the orange orb to guide him as the sea level began to rise and cover his path.

With every step and wave, his depression and rage multiplied and magnified. By the time he reached the lighthouse, he was boiling like the raging sea around him. He threw down his jacket and seethed as he paced back and forth, trying to find something to scream to the heavens. He picked up both wine bottles and thought about walking straight into the sea and never coming back, but the action didn't match the intensity of his intentions. He was on the edge of a psychotic break, and he wanted more. He didn't want to be muted. He wanted to convulse with a release of energy. Robert wanted a fight. Once he knew what he wanted, everything solidified. Like a concrete pile on his psyche, every negative, painful emotion and thought he had ever experienced calcified and pushed down on him. Once it had gained enough mass and pushed its entire weight upon his soul, he cracked. His psyche experienced a complete break.

He let out a primal scream to the ocean and shook his wine-filled fist at the heavens. "THROW ME TO THE SEA! THROW ME TO THE SEA!"

The shock of it exhilarated him. He didn't know exactly what he was screaming at, but he knew it was bigger than himself. It could have been the Heavens, the Universe with all the Gods in it, or some entity that represented his spiritual self. Although it dwarfed him, he didn't perceive inadequacy in its presence. He was a worthy opponent for anything the Universe could throw at him. With this newfound dogma, Robert was a man gone mad. He continued to scream, "If you've got nothing left for me, then throw me to the sea! You want me to admit defeat? You want me to admit I'm weak? I won't! If my life has to be written off, *I* won't do it for you! You want me, you come here, and you throw me to the sea!!!"

With that, a great wave broke over him. He was knocked off balance, but regained it quickly and smiled like a madman. He laughed and let out, "That's right! You come get me! Snuff me out if my whole life is meaningless! You made me; you do this! I'll endure a lifetime of pain if for nothing else than to rub it in your face!" Another wave crashed over him, but he was ready, and he steadied himself and broke it with all his force behind a shoulder.

"It won't be that easy!" Another wave crashed, and another came from the opposite direction. Each time, Robert braced for them. As the waves became more frequent, he began swinging punches at them, all the while holding his wine in his fists. The seawall was now ankle-deep with water and concealed from view. Robert couldn't go back to land if he wanted to. He looked like a lunatic, miles out in the middle of a raging sea, with two wine bottles in his hands while fighting the waves and taunting the Gods. He swung at them, tackled them, and took them head-on with a firm stance. All the while smugly drinking his wine. The contents of the bottle he had been drinking from became diluted with salt water, and with each breath, he took in spray from the waves. He thought he might finish drinking the bottles and go on to consume the sea. The waves became so fierce and steady that he could no longer shout at the sea, only fight it with muscles that were fortified with wine and sea water. He was raging like a prize fighter through twelve rounds.

A sudden pause in the fight threw Robert off guard. He stumbled a bit and then tried to find a solid footing. Before he could find his foundation, a huge black wave came down on him. He slid across the platform, but braced himself before falling into the deep water. He got to his feet and spotted the picnic table teetering over the edge. "No!" Robert shouted as he ran towards the table. "No! You came for me; you get nothing *but* me!" He overshot it and ran straight into the table with all his momentum. He doubled over the table, bear-hugged his arms around it, and began dragging it back to the middle of the seawall. "You get nothing!" he repeated. "Nothing but what you came for! If I'm not good enough, you admit it!"

A wave surged from beneath and upended the table. Robert took another wave against it. The table slammed into the bottle he was drinking from and shattered it. He knew it was mostly salt water and laughed at getting one over on the entity for not taking the bottle still full of wine. Robert shouted, "Fine! You get broken pieces!" He threw the broken neck in his hand against the lighthouse wall to shatter it to fine pieces; he wouldn't give the entity the satisfaction of destroying more of the bottle than he could. He would not let it get any credit for destruction tonight unless it was of his. He uncorked the second bottle, took a swig, and, realizing it was pure wine, he recorked it and held it close to his body as the assault prevailed. He pushed the table over so it would be upright in the middle of the plateau, jumped atop his great prize he plucked from the clutches of the sea, and shouted, "All you get is what I was given! If I'm too flawed for you to have me, then my point is proven! I'll mock you until the end! *Your* creation is flawed, *you* end it, not me!" He began stomping his feet on the table as more waves came as regularly as they did before and threatened to dismount him. Shells and rocks stirred up in the waves pelted his body in response. Seaweed wrapped around his ankles, trying to snare him. He fought every wave with the same energy as he fought the first ones. The sea never relented, and he never tired. He continued stomping and screaming, "You do it! YOU do it! YOU DO IT!!!"

The water pulled back and exposed the seawall and all the rocks and sand around it. The first glint of the early morning light on the horizon was blacked out by the enormous wave forming in the distance. For the first time that night, Robert tasted genuine fear before he fed it to his furnace and burned it for fuel. He waited until the wave began lurching forward, and with his timing right, he launched off the table and began running to meet it head on at the end of the seawall. He drove a shoulder into it and simultaneously punched at it with his fist that held the bottle. As the two crashed, Robert was lifted off his feet. The wine bottle connected with his temple, and the last thing he saw was one great blue flash before everything went black.

Robert regained consciousness as if shipwrecked. He was stretched out on the length of the picnic table and baking in the sun that was a white-hot orb behind the always overcast sky. He tried to find a footing in his faculties, but they also suffered as if they had been set out in the sun to cure. Although he didn't have a migraine, he had a severely aching spot on his temple where the bottle had struck it that was sensitive to the gentle heat of the sun. He sat upright and swung his legs over the side of the table as he took inventory of the wreckage. Pieces of dried kelp were baking into leather around him among the broken shells and rocks scattered across the end of the seawall. In a daze, he mindlessly scanned the debris until his eyes caught a gray rectangle that he recognized as Marie's book. Thankful that it wasn't lost to the sea, he went over to it to. As he stepped over the broken shells, his work pants were dry and stiff with salt, and his body was sore as he bent over. He fanned through the cockled pages; they were mostly dried, and he was relieved to see that the text was fine and readable. He carefully placed the book on the table to further dry. He removed the packs of cigarettes from his pockets. Two of them disintegrated in his hands, but the third had been protected enough by the cellophane that he thought the cigarettes may still be useable. He opened the pack and, finding that they were slightly damp and flattened, he placed them one by one on the table to fully dry. As he formed a concern about the wind blowing them, he realized the air was still.

 Robert turned his attention to the seascape. The sea's surface was as smooth as glass, and the wind was absent. The ships in the distance appeared lifeless and out of place. He carefully focused his ears and couldn't hear the familiar sound of the waves lapping against the rocks. He went down the side of the seawall to investigate where he saw the still water meeting the rocks. His mind couldn't make sense of it, and the sense of worry that should have taken hold of him had remained as still as the water. Still in a waking daze, he scanned the unusual shoreline and spotted his bottle of wine, half-submerged in the water and cradled by a bed of seaweed. He plucked it from the sea and observed the water drip down and ripple on the surface and then quickly fall in order with the surrounding stillness. He put a hand in the water to discern if it was real. The water was cool and refreshing. He knelt down, placed the bottle on the rocks, and began palming the seawater over his head. After his senses woke, he stood and looked out to the horizon. Robert had never experienced the doldrums. The still vastness before him was as refreshing as the cool water evaporating from his skin. He relished in rejuvenation. He took the bottle from among the rocks and held it up to the white orb, and he saw it was dark and mostly full. He uncorked it to be sure of its contents. The taste of pure wine, in contrast to the saltwater mixture from last night, exhilarated the rest of his senses. He recorked the bottle and brought it back to the table to place it among his other shipwrecked items. Robert then searched for his jacket and found it was washed up against the base of the lighthouse. He shook it out and spread it on the table to dry. Next to his jacket were twenty of Marie's surviving cigarettes, her book of poetry, and a decent amount of her wine. He plucked a lighter from his pocket, tested it a few times, and with the satisfaction of the dancing flame, he placed it next to the cigarettes. Much like the doldrums containing him, his mind was free of urgency. He decided if he was ever going to learn how to spend time with Marie in his mind, then this would be the perfect opportunity.

The pain in his temple turned his attention to the bottle and reminded him that a migraine was likely. He needed to drink the wine before the pain from last night caught up with him. He knew a hangover was pending like a departing train from a distant city, and he could only imagine how his body was going to react to the beating the waves worked over on him. After putting the bottle to lips, held the wine over the back of his tongue before finally swallowing. He recorked the bottle and looked at his world.

The doldrums were working as a spiritual shelter and amplifying the calmness of Robert's mind after he had reached a breaking point last night. The stillness purged his mind of the intense emotions that had reached devastating levels. He knew he only had a limited time to experience this peace before his mind would start the work of feeding his emotions. He exploited this rare opportunity of peacefulness and spent the afternoon out at the end of the seawall. He started a cigarette, and behind a long drag off it, he inhaled as deeply as he could before briefly holding the smoke and then emptying his lungs. With no wind, the smoke slowly rose until it joined the overcast sky. He uncorked the wine and folded its flavor into the taste of cigarette smoke. Fortified, he sat atop the table and began reading.

Over the next few hours, Robert found himself in a moment of perfect existence. He had no inclinations and simply *was*. His senses took in everything around him and uncategorizably accepted them with no form of analysis. The wine and cigarettes slalomed throughout his veins without putting him into any mood. He read the poetry without bias. Between bouts of reading, he walked every inch of his end of seawall and looked out into the world with a child-like sense of wonder. The factory skyline looked like a movie set. The ships signaled no threats of automation, and the endless horizon offered intoxicating possibilities of faraway places that were hidden just beyond the drop.

He was free from any expectations. For those few hours, he existed as if his entire life cycle would be unknown to history and overlooked by the universe. A humble existence with no expectations from any outside forces other than the unsolicited allowance to continue being. Robert looked out at the universe through the eyes of a spectator without cause for action. Despite the turmoil of his emotions boiling over the night before, the comedown from such a traumatic experience did not leave him with the usual numbing sense that his life was meaningless —he simply regarded his existence as curious and remained content to see his time on the wall through.

As the wine in the bottle slowly diminished down to its last sip, Robert began preparing for the journey home. He knew that the wine in his system would last long enough to protect him from any looming emotions or migraines, but it would be safer to brace himself, anyway. He donned his jacket, tucked Marie's book inside the pocket against his chest, and then zipped it tight for security. As he looked out at the water after smoking the last cigarette, he could sense his time in the doldrums was ending. Just before the horizon, he could make out a glimmer where the sea was coming back to life and returning to its natural rhythm. He cautiously watched it as he turned the bottle up and drank the last of its contents. With the empty bottle in his hand, he wished he were more inspired and had a pen and paper to send a message out to sea. Making do with what he had, he tore his favorite poem from the book and re-read it as he imagined himself the recipient of the cryptic message. He finished the cigarette, tucked Marie's book back in his jacket, and rolled the page of poetry into a cylinder before stuffing it down and recorking the bottle. He stood and looked out at the sea with the bottle in his hands while he collected himself and tried to put a cap on the significance of his experience. He imagined the bottle in flight and then breaking the surface of the water, setting off a reaction that would shatter the doldrums and bring reality tumbling down. It was an unsettling thought, and in response, he abandoned the romantic notion of a stranger finding the bottle and simply placed it in the lighthouse's doorjamb.

    The walk back to the mainland invited notions

of reality back into his mind. His heart rate quickened slightly and pumped the alcohol away from its numbing effects. The pain from where the bottle had struck began pulsating as a migraine fed off it from behind his eyes. Gently at first and then at a full gust, the wind returned, and the waves came back to life. He thought of last night and was irked at the fact that he still didn't know where everyone from The Bounty had gone. He looked down and pushed his fists further into his pockets. A slight tinge of rejection locked his jaw, and his usual disposition and abrasive attitude towards the world around him had taken hold by the time he made it on a train.

The buzzing lights on the train began evaporating any influence the alcohol had held in his mind. He wished he had sunglasses as he chose a spot on the floor to focus on for strength. He tried not to think about the rocking of the train or the strobing effect of the buildings flashing by the windows. The elements of the world around him began irritating his senses. He prepared himself for the fact that he would have to move to an empty part of the train if someone got too close to him; even if they didn't interact with him, their energy would charge him with anxiety. When the train mercifully came to rest at his station, he rushed out with his eyes locked on the ground until he reached his apartment.

Finally at home, Robert undressed and dropped onto his bed, where he fell into a hard, dreamless sleep before the migraine had a chance to fully take hold. He was able to embrace the void for a few hours before the pain woke him. In a type of fever-dream, he went in and out of consciousness as the pain ebbed and flowed. His body still pushed and pulled with phantom waves as the abstract visions of poetry pushed and pulled on his mind. In his delirium, he escaped the turbulence and found proper sleep that lasted a few more hours before the phone rang. The sound started in his forgotten dream and then pulled him into reality. He braced for pain but found that his sleep had defeated the migraine. With only a dull headache, he got up from his bed and put the receiver to his ear.

"Jack," he said, knowing it could only be him.

"Robert! Where have you been? Come down to The Bounty." Jack's voice seemed off, but Robert didn't want to question it.

"The last time I did, it was all boarded up," he said sarcastically as he continued to wake up and gain a sense of what time it was.

"Yeah, I'll tell you about that." Jack's voice turned stern. "We lost Frank. He died last night. Just get down here and I'll bring you up to speed." The room flashed brighter as Robert's pupils dilated in response to Jack's words. The shock flashed the pain of a migraine for a split second as Robert's heart throttled in his throat, and he set the receiver back in its cradle. He quickly dressed and made his way to the bar.

On his approach, he could see The Bounty was

shining like a neon beacon in the night. He had a strange sense of relief that, when it mixed with the news of Frank's death, unsettled him. As he got closer, he could sense the energy from the bar had a different frequency than he was used to. He braced himself against the strange energy as he swiftly passed the phone booth where he imagined a vulture perched like an ominous gargoyle. The sounds from within the bar grew louder at the entrance, and Robert a flash of the rejection from night before made itself known as he reached for the handle.

The door easily gave way this time. Instead of the usual rush of light and sound that overwhelmed him, the inside of The Bounty was set up like a wake. The mood was serious and sober as he cut through the somber crowd and joined Jack at the bar. A beer came his way, and he accepted it and drank it before speaking.

"Well, tell me." Robert did not know what to brace himself for, but his faculties were stable; the emotions that erupted last night allowed him to reset. He watched and waited for his response. Jack looked into his beer as he shook his head and drank. Robert remained silent. He knew Jack would tell him everything once he was able. Finally, after the two settled in, Jack confided in Robert.

"We were working on tomorrow's protest." Jack lowered his voice. "The plan was to shut off the water supply to the boilers. Once the boilers dry up by tomorrow, we're going to turn the water back on.

When the cold water hits the hot boilers, it's going to blow the place to hell."

Robert's mind snagged on something. "What do you mean *when* it hits? When it happens... as in you still plan to go through with it? Even after this?" Robert put out an open hand towards the bar full of mourners.

Jack simultaneously looked defeated and defiant. "Well, he can't have died for nothing!"

Robert saw the veins in Jack's neck grow tighter and backed off his line of questioning to focus on Frank. "You're right," he said, trying to reconnect with Jack. "How did it happen with Frank?"

Jack's eyes went searching. "We were in the factories after we cut off the water supply to make sure the boilers were all running on high. Frank caught sight of the automated machines; they were all out of their crates and fully assembled. It looked like they were ready to start work tomorrow if they hadn't already. Frank lost it. He grabbed a wrench and got himself worked up, and started beating one of the machines as hard as he could. He was doing what everyone wanted to do, so we kept watch for security and let him get it all out. He screamed at the machines, screamed at everyone around, and kept working the machine over with that wrench until suddenly everything went quiet. We thought a security guard got to him, so we rushed over. We found him on the ground. He had a heart attack and was dead before we got to him."

Jack's hands were shaking as he tried to light a cigarette. "We couldn't leave him there, otherwise someone might find out about the boilers. We knew there was no saving him, but we got him to a hospital anyway, just to make it respectful, I guess. At least he's not alone in the factories right now."

Robert couldn't think of anything to say. He decided it was best to say nothing and stay there in unity with Jack, but as the scene of Frank's death slowly faded from recent memory, Robert began looking around the bar, and his mind went back to the boilers. He tried to balance disappointment and sadness. He shook his head. "You're sure you're still going to go through with it tomorrow? None of this..." Jack cut him off.

"Robert... just leave it. It's too late. We're not getting into the politics of the thing. Frank is dead. We're here to mourn him tonight, and tomorrow we go through with the protest."

"You're going to gather everyone from the District and invite them to stand around while a bunch of boilers explode?"

Jack rubbed his head and drank his beer before venting his frustration. "They won't get hurt. The protest is far enough from the boilers that no one will be near them. The explosions won't even be big enough to have any influence on automation. We might delay it, but it's more about the display. The protest and the boilers should get enough coverage that if anything can be done about it, then the right people will get involved. If nothing else, it'll be a proper send-off for Frank."

It was a lot for Robert to take in. He didn't want to see any part of this plan go forward, but he knew it was too late for anything to be done about it. He tried not to assign emotion to it; it was something that was happening without him, whether or not he braced energy against it. He wished he were back in the doldrums. He drank his beer and settled in at The Bounty to comfort Jack as the impromptu memorial service took hold of the evening.

8

The sounds of the protest came in the late morning. Robert stirred from his bed and went out to his balcony to smoke and watch the event pass by; costumes, banners, and the sounds of drums and chants made it look more like a parade than a demonstration. As he scanned the faces, he wondered what aspects Marie had helped design. He saw more factory workers than he expected scattered throughout the younger crowd, but his eyes didn't lock on to anyone he recognized. There were no signs of Jack or his men, and he thought they were manipulating the water supply. He thought of their conversation last night and the anxiety of anticipation charged his skin as he thought of how the events would play out. He hoped Jack was right that the explosions would be far enough away that they wouldn't send the crowd into a panic. His stomach knotted as he looked at the people and his mind conjured up scenes of chaos.

Robert went back inside and showered to clear his mind and decide on what he should do. It was important to him to be a witness to the events that were going to play out on this day, but he still wanted to maintain his stance of not getting too involved. He didn't want to join the crowd and get mixed in with their movement or leave himself at the whims of mob mentality. The thought of calling Jack and being a witness from the factory side was also out of the question; he thought he was already in too deep just by knowing what they were planning. He wouldn't allow himself to be embedded within the destruction without being fully committed to their views. Robert sighed and let the water run down his face while he abandoned any inclinations and waded in the temporary comfort of detachment.

Without knowing his intentions, Robert knew he would go stir crazy if he stayed in his apartment. He scrubbed his face and turned up the heat as he played with the possibility of leaving town. The idea of leaving everything behind brought a sense of relief. The protest and the boilers would be enough of a distraction for him to leave unnoticed, and he thought it might even be a few days before anyone realized he was gone. He could live without his few possessions. The prospect of the entire world being at his disposal charged him with excitement. He played out the fantasy of going to Marie—she had left a forwarding address inscribed in the front cover of the book of poetry. He fantasized about enrolling in the same college as her and planning a settled-down life free of the politics and uncertainties of industry. He dreamed of stability and comfort.

He dried off and dressed, still fantasizing about ending up somewhere else in the world, but the realities of his life soon set in. If he left, he would need work, and with his luck, he would find himself mixed up with another group of people that were either content to waste away in the factories or determined to fight the eventuality of automation. He thought of automation catching up with him everywhere he went and wondered how long he could jump from factory to factory before he ran out of work. His mind drifted as he imagined factories consuming the Earth and began philosophizing about the state of automation. He considered whether the world would be a better place if people were free from work or if it would create a dystopian future of poverty for the working class.

Fully dressed, he decided he couldn't predict the future any better than he could flesh out his fantasies. He decided that if they were going to be the same everywhere he went, then he might as well watch the eventualities of his life play out in the next few hours and find out what options he would be left with. He left his apartment to trail behind the protestors, intending to study the crowd while retaining a non-committed distance of indifference.

With the worries of his own future left behind in his apartment, the thought of the boilers weighed heavily on Robert's mind. He chain-smoked cigarettes on the walk to the train station while trying to come up with a justification for the action. He could wrap his mind around the idea of the boilers to avenge Frank's death, but in terms of protest, he couldn't find a place in his mind for it to comfortably sit. The conflict wrestled in his mind and became too distracting; he wanted to keep his mind in the present moment so that he could react quickly. He purged his conflicting views out of his mind with the flick of a cigarette butt and watched them disperse on the asphalt with a red flash.

Inside the station, he lingered and waited for the last of the protestors to board before he walked along the platform to wait for the next train. The space retained the energy of the crowd that had just passed through and pushed Robert's mind to search for thoughts. Overlooking the empty tracks, he took on a somber mood at the thought of going to the factories without them being in full swing. He didn't like to see them without their energy and was hesitant to board the next train when it arrived at the station. As it stopped in front of him and opened its doors, Robert had one last fleeting thought of leaving town before boarding.

In the empty train car, Robert rode down the line while focusing his hearing, as if trying to infer sacred knowledge from the sounds coming to him. If he couldn't figure things out, he thought maybe the surrounding structures could. He couldn't expect to receive direct instructions, but he supposed the sounds might instill a mindset that would guide him. Robert rocked and swayed with the train car, trying to fall in rhythm with its frequency, but it had no influence on his mental state.

At his destination, the crowd had already departed and left the station empty. Reluctantly, Robert traversed the abandoned vault. The energy of the crowd reverberated stronger throughout the echoing chamber. He tried to absorb the energy from the walls and use it to steel his nerves. He placed an unlit cigarette between his lips as he reached the stairs and braced himself to be greeted by the factories.

Up on the street, the factory walls took on a different role as they echoed the noise from the distant protest. The sound of people was strange compared to the manufacturing sounds that usually accompanied the intimidating sight of the Brutalist structures. Robert didn't like the effect and was unsettled that the factories weren't active. He started his cigarette as he tried to place his thoughts. The factories seemed to him like a counterfeit representation of themselves that didn't accurately portray their role in society. He kept his head down and walked by them with indifference.

Robert turned the corner out of the abandoned corridor to the scene of a festival. The police had barricaded three sides of the intersection, leaving only the exit in the direction of the train station. The cops stood in force with stern expressions chiseled on their faces. The protestors looked festive, but the energy and tension told a different story. Robert kept his distance, but was close enough to make out the chants and general attitude of the demonstration. He remained wary of the two previous clashes this group had had with the police and hoped there would be no more violence. He planted his feet and stood firm, but kept his edge and was ready to move at the first sign of trouble. If the demonstration turned violent, he knew his factory-worker image wouldn't save him this time, with so many of his co-workers involved. He was not inclined to fight their fight, yet couldn't turn his back to any of what he was watching.

Robert's attention kept trying to fixate on all the aspects of the demonstration that would indicate peace. He wanted to convince himself that the protest was going to be as trivial as he had argued, yet his mind sensed the tension in the air and started going over a plan to escape. He looked back towards the way he came and decided that if things got out of hand that he could get to the trains before the wave of violence could catch him.

Of all the fantasizing Robert had done, and of all the possibilities he had played out, he was not prepared for the events that unfolded. Living among industry, there was always a background noise given off by the factories. It was a slow hum and reverberation that ran through all the buildings and energized the people. Sitting still, one was aware of the low vibration running through their body. Robert thought of it as the same sensation as putting his hand around a pipe and being able to tell if it had water running through it, but the energy from the factories could be sensed throughout his whole body and affect his mind. Suddenly, every energized atom in Robert's body stood still. The ground solidified, and the air lost its electric charge. The intensity of life was dulled. Robert knew it was the boilers that had exhausted the last of their water; they had finally been choked of their supply and lay dormant as the fires burned under them and continued to heat them. The crowd became unsettled by the sense that something was happening in the same primal way that animals can sense an earthquake. Over the next few moments, the crowd's chants were reduced to a murmur. Robert was sick with anticipation as he braced himself for the distant explosions and kept looking back at his exit as the crowd became unpredictable. The pit in Robert's stomach became a painful knot in his gut the longer he waited, but the explosions were delayed. Instead, the noise he heard was the astonishment of the crowd. With no steam being released by the boilers, the overcast sky cleared. The vapor thinned out and then opened a hole in the canopy above the protestors to reveal the blue sky and the midday sun shining down on them.

Robert looked up with wonder. He couldn't remember the last time he had seen the blue sky. He had almost forgotten it existed and accepted the overcast sky as a permanent fixture. A hush fell over the crowd as everyone looked up as if receiving a gift from the Gods. But the moment of awe was only temporary as the absence of energy from the boilers was replaced by the cosmic energy radiating from the sun. The protest regained its momentum and then surpassed it. The sun shining down on a crowd of people that hadn't seen it for years was too much for them to manage. They erupted in savagery. The crowd went mad as the solar energy penetrated their skulls and possessed their minds. The protest turned into a frenzy. The police, driven just as mad by the sunlight as the crowd, responded with the same frenzied energy. The protest began taking on the form of a riot as the crowd began shouting louder and throwing projectiles at the cops and factories. They broke factory windows and tore down anything they could dismantle. Tear gas was shot at the maddening crowd, which only responded with an escalation of violence.

Robert couldn't believe his eyes—he not only saw the cops and protestors openly fighting in the streets, but also the protestors fighting among themselves. Robert's feet froze and wouldn't allow him to flee as he watched in amazement as the melee played out. A shock of horror seized him as the momentum of the scene shifted and the police barricades were broken through. The bedlam broke the dam and began rushing down the street towards the factories. Robert had never had an exact layout of Jack's plan, but the crowd was running towards the center of the hole in the sky, and he knew that's where the boilers must have been cut off from their water supply. Robert couldn't flee the terror and let the crowd run to their deaths; he had to warn them. He had to get to the front of the crowd to either tell them about the danger they were heading towards or to influence the direction of the crowd and lead them away from the boilers.

Robert ran as fast as he could through the gauntlet of tear gas and violence. He took a few glancing blows from billy clubs that were intended for other targets and narrowly avoided tear gas canisters that went screaming by his head. He ran with his neck stretched high, trying to find the front of the hoard. He was pushed off balance by a fight that had rumbled into his path and stumbled over the wreckage in the streets. It was as if he was fighting the waves again. He shouted about the boilers as he made his way into the main body of the crowd, but it was as futile as shouting at the sea; the crowd had become an entity that had taken on a life of its own. He lost cognizant control of his actions and continued running and shouting in futility until his heart jolted.

The only person he had recognized all day had just flashed before him. The crowd had made it into a train yard where the freight cars unloaded their cargo, and he caught a flash of Lucy before she disappeared again behind another car. If he couldn't stop everyone, he could at least save her. He ran to the train cars and made it into their maze just as the first explosion came. It started as a loud hiss that turned into a rumble and then released all its energy with a loud cracking blast. A deadening thud manipulated the air out of Robert's chest as realized the intensity of the explosion. He also realized Jack's plan; the boilers must have been in the factories that surrounded the train yard. Disabling the train yard would halt the distribution of the automated machines and create the disturbance that the driver's strike had tried to accomplish.

Sweat trickled off Robert's temple as he came to terms with just how deadly the situation had become. The frenzied crowd was unaware of the severity of the explosion, and instead of scaring them out of their pandemonium, the blast only frenzied them further. Robert ran through the cars, searching for Lucy as more explosions rocked the train yard. The hole in the sky filled again with the dust from the destruction, but the sun had already done its work, and the crowd showed no signs of calming. They were trying to destroy everything, as if they were working with the boilers to take down every brick of industry.

Robert finally locked eyes with Lucy. She looked afraid, and he was relieved to see that she was having a normal response to the chaos and knew he could coax her away from danger. He ran towards her and grabbed her by the shoulders. He could not calm her, but he saw she recognized him. Robert knew the boilers were only an isolated event, and if they could just make it out of the train yard, they would be safe. He had no delusion that he could convey all of that to Lucy, but it didn't matter. She put up no resistance as he grabbed her wrist to lead her away.

Under the frenzied noise, a slow, high-pitched whistle, unlike the other noises that built up to the explosions, began to gain momentum. It sent a chill up Robert's spine as it became deafening. A boiler in the factory had failed to function in accordance with the plan. Instead of exploding, the boiler's pipes broke off and created a focused release of energy. The boiler lurched forward, broke off its mounts, and rocketed through a factory wall with a deafening crack. It lost no momentum as it shot through the train yard before finally slamming into the side of the train car that Robert and Lucy were running behind. The sound of the boiler colliding with the car deafened and confused Robert. He tried to find an equilibrium as his ears rang. The boiler hit the train car with so much force that it lifted it up at an angle. The car slowly lurched and threatened to fall over on its side. Steam continued to surge out of the back of the boiler as its relentless pressure further pushed the car over. As Robert gained enough of a bearing to locate Lucy in relation to the looming threat, the shadow of the car grew out in front of him and engulfed them. He gathered all his strength in the same way the great wave had shown him the night before, springing forward to shove Lucy as hard as he could. He cleared her from danger and clambered backwards on the gravel just as the train car dropped on him.

Robert was crushed from the waist down under the car. The ringing in his ears went silent, and his peripheral vision became tunneled. The last boiler to explode was the one that had toppled the train car. Pinned to the ground, Robert saw nothing but the sky as it cleared again and came to life with the dancing of the blue-sky sprites. As his vision became more tunneled, the sprites became more vivid. Instead of shooting in and out of existence, they became more consistent and swirled from their place high in the sky down to meet Robert. Robert experienced nothing other than their energy running through his body as each individual sprite that passed through him removed a malevolent aspect from his spirit. The procession of sprites swirled through him, removing every negative aspect of the human condition until he was left in a state of ecstasy. He was weightless. The pressure of the world that he had known so intimately was finally removed from his psyche. The sprites then encompassed him and slowly lifted him to the sky. Rising to the heavens, his tunneled vision concentrated to a single, electrified bright point before it burst with a brilliant blue flash.

9

Marie rode the train in a state of exhaustion. Although she was awake, her mind fell into rhythm with the frequency of sleep and began accessing memories of dreams long forgotten. They kept flashing in and out of her memory. It fascinated her to an extent; if she had to sit and list any dreams that she could remember, she would not be able to recall most of them. But as she rode the train, dreams going as far back as her childhood kept appearing in her memory as if she had lived through them only last night. As she recalled every detail of a dream she had as a child, she tried to decipher its meaning. She tried to understand why her mind would carry something outside of her reach for so long, only to display it years later, but the exercise only exhausted her faculties further.

Her waking memories, in contrast, were like incomplete dreams. She had not slept well for the last few weeks, as she was unable to get the full story out of anyone. It had been over a week since Lucy had called her—more than a week had passed after Robert had died before Lucy had been able to pick up the phone and speak. From the time that Marie had heard about the events that led to his death, she had been stressed. She did not know who had gotten hurt or died or who was still living among the factories. When Lucy spoke to her, she was back home living with her parents. The events traumatized her and scared her parents into pulling her out of school. Anyone Marie tried to contact either had very few details to offer or were gone and impossible to get hold of.

    Marie broke through the image of a dream that her mind had projected on the train's window. The scene outside over the last few hours had turned from an open natural landscape to suburban development, and now the factories and industrialized land began consuming everything in sight and lazily stretched out to the horizon. Her detached mind imagined the processes within; she conjured up a giant roll of sheet metal unwinding down a conveyor belt. A large sharp guillotine came down at regular intervals to cut the metal into workable lengths. Down a labyrinth of conveyors, the metal was manipulated and shaped by an army of automated machines. They cut, folded, welded, and ground away at the metal until it took the shape of a box. The engraving on the box showed Robert's name. It slid down the conveyor and was pushed onto different tracks until it reached the end of the line. The barcode was scanned, and then another machine's arm came down and placed the box under a device that deposited Robert's ashes into their receptacle. Robert's ashes went down the line, where they joined hundreds of indigent remains of people who had died in the county and had no one to claim them.

Marie's throat tightened with anxiety. After she had finally gotten the story out of Lucy, she was determined to get to Robert's ashes before they were bulldozed into a communal grave. It was the least she could do; she knew Robert would mark her mind for the rest of her life. When she thought of him, she wanted to know joy, and she decided that if she let his ashes fall into that forgotten grave, her memories of him would be eclipsed by grief and regret. She checked her watch and reassured herself that she would make it in time. She noted that the train had now carried her deep into industry and that if she were running late, the sky would have already begun to transform from gray overcast to the churning, bright orange sky of the industrial night.

Looking at the sky, she watched the steam and pollution pouring out of the smokestacks. She thought how the fumes from Robert's cremation must have been exhausted up into the sky and joined the constantly churning entity. It depressed her to think of him as being part of the barrier that had blocked the stars from him for so long. She turned her attention to the notification on the screen by the doors that indicated her station was the next stop.

Out on the street, Marie quickened her pace in the crematorium's direction. Her anxiety would not diffuse until she safely had Robert's ashes in her possession. Panic excited her mind at the sound of what she thought was the engine of a bulldozer behind the cemetery's fence. She rushed through the doors and quickly made it to the counter. She had no time to explain to the funeral director about her relationship with Robert. She lied and said she was family. The director didn't give her explanation enough time to decide whether he believed it. He had been busy since the protest. Beginning with Frank's body and then those of some protestors and workers, including Robert's, he was at his wit's end. His usual business was to process the remains of a few old workers that had finally died of hard lives or the occasional workplace accident. His business had consumed him since the tragedy, and he was happy to find someone to offload one of his worries onto. With a quick exchange of signatures and paperwork, Robert's ashes were passed to Marie. The anxiety washed out of her mind, and with relief she welcomed the sadness that came with the reality of Robert's death.

From the crematorium, Marie set out on a funeral procession that took her on the same route that she and Robert had followed out to the seawall. The streetlights and Brutalist buildings were watching respectfully as she walked the streets and drank from a bottle of wine. The way she carried her sadness transformed her into a majestic reality; instead of her emotions breaking her, their pressure fortified her. She walked the streets with somber strength and purpose throughout the industrial city until she made it to the sea.

Marie ended her journey sitting on the table at the end of the seawall under the overcast sky. The ships had since cleared out; after the protest, the process of automation swiftly took over and removed most of the people from the equation. With the strikers and protestors out of the way, the boats quickly unloaded their cargo and returned to the various ports of the world. Marie watched the open sea as she smoked a cigarette and continued to drink from the bottle of wine. The nondescript metal box that contained Robert's ashes lay next to her on the table. She had hoped that the patch of stars would eventually peek out from behind the horizon and that she could share them with Robert one last time.

As the sky darkened, the streetlight above the table glowed and buzzed with life. Marie's eyes picked up on a glimmer that she hadn't noticed before. She went to the door of the lighthouse and found the bottle that Robert had left. She held it up to the streetlight to examine its contents and saw there was something inside. Back at the table, she uncorked the bottle and slid a finger down its neck to retrieve the message. Once unrolled in the light, she recognized it as one of the poems from the book that she had given Robert. Her heart raced as she realized he must have been out here with her on his mind. Her mind tried to destroy the notion of time and imagine that they were sitting and reading on the table together.

Marie read the poem several times through Robert's filter and decided on his proper send off.

She opened the box on the table, removed the bag that contained his ashes, and carefully poured them into the empty bottle. She then rolled the poem back up and sent it down with the ashes. As a final gift, she withdrew a cigarette. While she drank her wine and thought of Robert, she slid the cigarette across her bottom lip after every sip until the wine had fully stained it. She conjured images of Robert and held on to them as long as her mental strength would allow. As her faculties neared the edge of complete exhaustion, she then dropped the wine-laced cigarette into the bottle and recorked it.

Marie stood at the end of the seawall with Robert's ashes in her hands as she reflected on what she knew of his life. She thought of him in the factories with the sterile influence of industry constantly infiltrating his mind and emotions and how he turned his experience into insights that she never would have arrived at on her own. She regarded him as something beautiful that she wanted to bear witness to. She imagined a life with him, and thought of how they were supposed to continue their lives through each other's filters until they finally reached a consensus. Although they may have never seen each other again, knowing that he was out in the world would have helped her see things through his eyes. As she stood alone, she knew how much work it was now going to be on her own.

She was saddened that Robert had only known the factories. She had shown him the stars on their first date, but she wished she could have shown him more. With his ashes in her hands, she was going to throw him to the sea and give him the gift of the world. She hoped he would travel every inch of the sea and experience the rest of history through a spiritual rush of emotion.

She saw the stars finally reveal themselves and wanted to shed a tear for him, but none would come. She was going to face Robert's end as bluntly as she could manage and try to record every detail with elegant reverence so that she may return to this place in her mind as a moment that would put her world in perspective. She pulled back and threw the bottle as far as she could towards the horizon. In that instant, the wind picked up, and the sea retreated to expose a flat spot where a rock nearly breached the surface. A bolt of terror struck her heart. The bottle dropped from its flight and burst on the rock with a deadening thud before the sea rushed in to claim Robert.

-Andy James-
FlameSkyNight@gmail.com

Made in the USA
Columbia, SC
13 May 2023